# SAY GOODBYE TO HOLLYWOOD

Jenny Trout

This book is dedicated to everyone who had a laugh reading my *Fifty Shades of Grey* recaps, to everyone who bought *The Boss*, to everyone who has had fun with me on this journey. You're the best supporters any blogger could hope for.

## Chapter One

The cover of Lynn Baldwin's debut novel, *Beautiful Darkness*, bears the words, "#1 *New York Times* Bestseller" and "Over 100 Million Copies Sold!". In the glossy image, a necklace of red beads drapes over a black lacquered surface, presumably the piano the tortured hero of the story, Damian Bennet, has played since he was a boy. A twenty-nine-year-old internet billionaire and underground mixed martial arts competitor, Damian meets naive, virginal college student Ella Vaughn on page five and, through four-hundred-sixty-eight pages of flowery humping and alarmingly violent personal altercations, their destinies and hearts are forever changed.

The cover art is tasteful. The story, not so much.

I take a long, deep breath and hold it until the elevator arrives and the doors open. A short, pale woman holds the open-door button and leans slightly forward to address me. "Jessica Yates?"

I want to extend my hand, but all I can think is that she'll release the button, and my arm will be trapped between the closing doors "Yes. And you're Kathy?"

"Kathy Muller, yes." She gestures me into the elevator with her. "Lynn is so excited to meet you."

"I'm looking forward to it." I take another deep breath and slowly exhale with the climbing floors.

"What did you think of the book?" Muller asks, a twinkle in her eyes. It matches the twinkle in the eyes of the women at yoga when they mention the book, and the eyes of the clerk at the bookstore where I purchased a copy.

The correct answer to a twinkler is, of course, positive, even if my opinion of the book is not. "It's like nothing I've ever read before."

She beams at me. Like Lynn Baldwin, Kathy Muller is from Oklahoma. In fact, she's Baldwin's cousin; that's how she got the job as Lynn's assistant in the first place.

I stare down at the book in my shaking hands.

Sure, I think it's terrible. The storyline is needlessly convoluted; what dotcom billionaire had time for underground fighting rings? Why, if the heroine is so afraid of BDSM, does she make a bet to become his submissive? The writing itself comes off stilted and juvenile, and the much-vaunted sex scenes read like the protagonists are having asthma attacks, instead of orgasms.

There are so many ellipses.

But one-hundred-million customers can't be wrong, can they? The book is a world-wide phenomenon. The last thing I wrote did well, but not *Forbes* well.

Lynn Baldwin was on the cover last month.

I glanced sideways at Kathy. She watches the numbers like we're at the stock exchange. Her gaze flicks to me. She smiles reassuringly and says, "We're almost there."

Though Macrocosm Studios' production offices are in Burbank, today, I'm at the Beverly Wilshire, where Mrs. Baldwin has been living during pre-production. She has to be on hand for the numerous components of the film she has unprecedented control over.

When it comes to *Beautiful Darkness*, everything is unprecedented. The bidding war for the film rights reached into the mid-seven figures. And, now, Macrocosm is sending me in for her approval. If this meeting goes well, I'll be adapting the current bestselling book in the world for a major motion picture.

This is a big deal for me. A huge deal, with a whole lot on the line. I'm in demand, now, but that demand will wane if I can't maintain commercial success. So far, my work has been acclaimed, but I've never really "popped". *Beautiful Darkness* might give me the boost I need to keep the phone ringing.

The elevator dings, and Muller announces, "Penthouse. Please, follow me."

It's not magnificent talent that's gotten me to the penthouse suite. I know the man to thank for getting me this meeting.

Jack Martin waits just inside the foyer. Whenever I hear the phrase "ruggedly handsome", I immediately picture Jack. He has the square jaw of a hardboiled detective in a comic strip and eyes like the youngest member of a boy band, and he looks like he could wear plaid shirts and survive in the wilderness. It's easy to see how he got his start in action movies.

He turns to me with his signature scary frown. I've been told that I have Resting Bitch Face. Jack has Resting If-You-Say-Another-Stupid-Word-So-Help-Me-God-I-Will-Throw-You-Off-A-Balcony face. It looks good on movie posters, but if you don't know him, it's incredibly intimidating in real life. Especially now that he's in his early forties, and his default expression has gone from "beer-fueled, Boston-born Irishman who just overheard you praising the Yankees", to "cold, distant father in a 1960s-set coming-of-age movie". And most especially when he's dressed like the *GQ* angel of death in a black suit, black shirt, and no tie. He turns, scratches his short brown hair, and greets me with, "I'm waiting for Ms. Baldwin."

The assistant at my side makes a strained polite face. "As I said before, she's making an appearance via satellite."

Jack rolls his eyes. I don't blame him. He's not the most important man in Hollywood, but he *is* important. He'd made Macrocosm a killing starring as a Russian sleeper agent in their *Dangerous Identity* franchise, and the first feature he produced for them had been an award-season darling. Jack Martin's name attached to anything is gold, but clearly, Lynn Baldwin has the same idea about herself.

Kathy hurries off, leaving us both to stand in the marble-walled foyer. "How long have you been waiting?"

"Longer than I should have," is the only answer he gives. He glances sideways at me. "You look nice today."

There's a mirror across the hallway to our right. I sneak a peek to make sure the back of my cream-colored blazer isn't tucked into my slacks or something. I'm wearing my favorite shirt beneath it, a dusky mauve silk blouse that brings out the "English rose" in my complexion. I do look pretty good. Maybe Jack wasn't being sarcastic.

I straighten the chain of the Jason Wu necklace I borrowed from one of my more fashionable friends and say, "Thanks?"

Jack has never once commented on my appearance while on the clock. Which means he's trying to boost my confidence. Which means he can tell I'm nervous.

Shit.

Kathy bustles back in and gives us a way-too-enthusiastic smile. "All right, thank you so much for waiting. She will see you, now."

Jack makes an "after you" motion, and I follow Kathy down the hall, into a spacious living room with a panoramic view. A large photo backdrop of L.A. dominates most of the room, and blazing camera lights click off one-by-one as a technician takes them down. Someone else is packing away a camera and cables.

"Just ignore them," Kathy says with a wave of her hand that implies she's taking it all in stride on just another day.

But Muller hasn't always been Baldwin's assistant, and Baldwin hasn't always lived this life.

Kathy takes us to a smaller media room with wood paneling and a sleek television in a modern white shelving unit.

"Ms. Baldwin will be just one more moment," she assures us, then draws the wood divider across the wide doorway like a bowing footman.

"Christ, it's like we're here to meet the Pope," Jack says, and he makes a noise that I've come to decode as a wry laugh.

There's one very modern armchair and an L-shaped sofa with evenly spaced throw pillows. I sit on one side, Jack sits on the other, and we both stare silently at the glass-topped coffee table that's nearly bumping our knees.

I've worked in Hollywood for the past fourteen years, and the only other time I was this nervous going into a meeting was when I was still in awe of Jack. He's nervous today, too. It's hard to tell, but since I've worked with him enough, I can see the signs. He's trying hard not to jiggle his knee, and he keeps taking a breath like he's going to say something then never does.

It feels like we've been waiting an eternity when the partition slides open again, and there she is. Soccer mom turned literary superstar, Lynn Baldwin.

Lynn is in her mid-forties and is a little overweight. Her long casual pink sweater and white leggings combo gives the impression that success hasn't removed her far from her comfortable suburban life in Oklahoma, but the sweater is cashmere, and no housewife I've ever seen wears diamonds the size of the one her left hand.

I assume it's an upgraded wedding ring, not the original.

"Jack! So good to see you again!" she exclaims, and I'm instantly relieved that she's as warm and personable as she is in interviews.

I stand at the same time Jack does, waiting in my spot while he rounds the coffee table to shake her hand and give her the customary air kiss beside her cheek.

"L.A. is agreeing with you," he says, turning on the charming smile that's made him *People*'s Sexiest Man Alive twice.

Ms. Baldwin pats her blond hair and demurs, "Oh, stop it. I feel like I'm getting such a big head since I came out here."

I'm glad she didn't greet me right away, because I'm in a little bit of shock trying to reconcile her appearance with the pictures I saw on the internet. Many of them were a month or more old, from her massive North American book tour. Her face isn't as lined as it was in those pictures, and her haircut and highlights are flawless, now. She turns to me and extends her hand; the four gold bangles on her wrist clink softly.

"Hi there, Ms. Baldwin. I'm Jessica Yates." I take her hand and shake it, and she uses this gesture to pull me in.

"Oh, please, call me Lynn." She looks as though she's about to say something else when she notices the copy of her book in my hands. I don't know why I'm still holding it. She takes it from me, sighing as though she's seeing it for the first time. "I love this cover. Don't you love this cover?"

"Much better than the one you used on your website," Jack says, and my spine stiffens. The self-published origins of *Beautiful Darkness* have been a touchy subject in interviews. Jack has to know that, right? He always does his homework.

Lynn's smile flickers and freezes for just a moment, then she laughs a little too loudly and says, "Well, let's not even talk about that."

"Right!" I jump in. "We're here to talk about the screenplay."

"It's exciting, isn't it?" she gushes, taking the armchair. Jack and I sit down, as well. Lynn draws one leg up beneath the other and rubs her hands together as she addresses me. "I'm sure Jack has already told you that this isn't going to be the usual arrangement. Macrocosm has offered me a lot of creative involvement, and I want to do right by my fans. I need to know that you're as committed to this story as I am."

My gaze flicks to Jack. He's lounging comfortably with one elbow on the back of the couch, and I see the sadistic little glimmer in his eyes. He knows how I feel about the book. When we first discussed the possibility of me writing the screenplay, I told him it would make a better psychological thriller than a hot-and-heavy romance.

The diplomatic statement I rehearsed on the drive over rolls out easily. "You know, I found something so compelling about this story. While I read it, I could see the movie in my mind. Do you ever read a book and just get that feeling, that spark, that there's more story to be told? Layers that you can't give to the reader in words but something that has to be shown visually?"

She nods, her expression composed and serious. I wonder, for a minute, if I offended her by suggesting there was something missing from her novel, but the corners of her eyes squint a little, and she says, "You know, when I was writing it, it looked like movie in my head."

I know this already, and so does Jack, because Lynn Baldwin has never kept it secret that a young, muscle-bound Jack Martin, fresh off his second spy movie, was the inspiration for Damian. I watch Jack shift just a little in his seat, and I have to keep myself from laughing.

"So, we're on the same page, then?" I ask. "No pun intended."

Pun totally intended. Jack hates them, and I like to antagonize him.

"Can you tell me some of what we'd be doing? I've never written a movie before, so I don't know what should stay or go or if anything really should go." Lynn looks from me to Jack.

He clears his throat, and I almost don't hear it over the alarm bells in my head. Has someone told Lynn that she'll be writing the screenplay *with* me? Jack never mentioned that.

"Right now isn't the time to talk about cuts to the work," Jack says. "I think the important thing we should discuss is tone. What *kind* of a film are we going to bring to the audience?"

"A hot one, I hope!" Baldwin says with an ear-splitting laugh. It's clear that she wants me to agree with her, but I have reservations. Since I read the first of the many sex scenes in the novel, I've been worrying about how to get whips and chains past the MPAA.

I try not to disagree with her outright. Today is all about getting her approval, so she'll give Jack the word that it's okay for me to proceed.

My answer is a cautious one. "Hot, definitely. We don't want to lose the sex appeal. But we want to make sure it doesn't come across as too explicit. I want viewers to focus on the love story."

"Of course, but the sex is such a visceral part of what—" She's interrupted by the divider opening, and a flash of truly alarming annoyance crosses her face. I make a mental note of that for later. If she has a quick temper, I don't want to be on the wrong side of it.

The man who enters is tall and lanky, with a bald head that reminds me of the shiny, pale surface of an egg bagel. He leans down to give Lynn a kiss on the forehead and tells her, "I'm taking the kids to the pool. Give me a call when you're finished here?"

"Absolutely, baby," she purrs back at him, and without an introduction, he's gone. She turns to us, a naughty glimmer in her eyes, and says, "Mr. Inspiration."

"Your husband?" Jack asks. I want to smack him.

"No, her au pair." My snark earns a big laugh from Lynn, but it doesn't unburden me from the knowledge that Damian Bennett is apparently some hellish mix of Lynn's husband in Jack's body.

"Oh, I like you," Lynn says, as though this is the ultimate compliment. "You're sassy. I think we'll get along very well."

"Jessica is one of the hardest working screenwriters Macrocosm has ever hired," Jack says, and winks at me. "But she is a lot of fun to work with."

Lynn's gaze shifts between the two of us, the corners of her eyes crinkling with piqued interest. Of course, the woman who wrote the bestselling romance novel of all time would jump to a romantic conclusion, but it still brings up all sorts of icky feelings that I thought I left in the past. There's nothing romantic between Jack and me. At least, not anymore.

Lynn studies me. "You're very familiar with my book, aren't you?"

"Absolutely. I couldn't put it down." I literally couldn't. I had to read it before this meeting. I take my copy and flip through the pages. "I even made notes in the margins."

Hopefully, she doesn't ask to read them. I could kick myself for bringing them up.

"What was your favorite part?" From Lynn's tone and the subtle freeze of her perfect suburban smile, I know this is a test.

This isn't my first rodeo. I've never adapted a sure-fire Hollywood blockbuster, but I know all about writer egos. I have my own. By the time I'm done working on this script, I'll have told her thirty "favorite" scenes I have. "When Damian interrupts the fight between Ella and Cassidy."

Something akin to relief crosses Lynn's face. If I were in her position, I would test people, too. It's easy for people to flatter you, but there's no guarantee of substance behind it. She shakes her head. "Don't you just hate Cassidy?"

Do I hate her, or am I supposed to hate her? The bitchy blond next-door neighbor who constantly taunts Ella grows tiresome within a few chapters. "I think we can have a lot of fun with that dynamic."

That dynamic won't make it into the final script, if I can help it. It's extraneous; Cassidy disappears around the mid-point of the novel and never reappears, with absolutely no explanation.

"I think this is a good fit," Jack says, too suddenly. It probably doesn't strike Lynn as desperate, because from anybody else, it wouldn't be. But my eyes go wide, like I just caught someone stuffing a body into a dumpster. Jack never tries to close out a meeting with a definite answer. It's his power move; he walks away and gives them the illusion that the ball is in their court. He wants this for me.

"Oh, I think you're absolutely right," Lynn agrees, and looks to me expectantly. "So, when can I see a script?"

My brain whirls. I want this job. I want the money. I want the security. I want whatever is on the other side of the door that this job will open for me. But I'm not sure I want to spend the next three or four months of my life immersed in the extremely narrow world of Damian and Ella.

Then, I look at Jack.

I owe this man everything. He's never steered me wrong once. Without him, the door to Hollywood would never have opened to me. Or maybe it would have, but certainly not in the way it had when it was Jack's hand on the doorknob.

As Lynn Baldwin, the Jacqueline Susann of her time, waits with her photo-ready benevolent smile, I ask, "Does this mean I have your approval to go forward?"

She animates with joy. "Of course, you do! Do you have any idea how many men the studio heads have had in here, talking to me about my book and how they *understand* it?" Lynn scoffs and throws a pointed sideways glance at Jack. "I can't trust a man to understand Ella the way a woman can. You know, a reporter said to me recently, 'Every woman sees herself in Ella Vaughn, no matter her age or her background,' and I think that's true. Ella is every woman, and only a woman can really live through her experiences."

"The reporter, wasn't that Brian Chambers for the *L.A. Times*?" Jack asks, deadpan.

I ignore him. "Well, I'm very excited. I'm sure there are things that need to be worked out with Jack and the studio—" I hope he hears the cash registers *ka-ching*ing in my head.

The sliding wall opens, and Kathy peeks in.

"Naturally," Jack cuts me off. "But let's save that. I think we've gone over our time."

"Oh, that's right. I have so many meetings and appearances today." Lynn stands, and Jack and I follow suit. Jack reaches over and gives Lynn a hearty handshake, but when it's my turn, she locks her fingers around mine and squeezes, her face contorting with emotion. "You're the right fit for this. I can feel it."

Instantly, I feel like an asshole. This woman believes in me. She trusts me to bring her vision to the screen. Writing is intimate. It's raw. It's daunting. And it's terrifying. I've been viewing her as someone beneath me, as a means to an end. I came into this meeting so full of myself, so derisive about her book.

I have to do better.

We leave, Kathy making all sorts of apologies. She walks us straight to the elevator, her eyes on our every move like we're fans who'll hide out somewhere in the penthouse. I almost want to snap that we're not going to steal Lynn's underwear. As we wait for the elevator, Kathy collects a toned blond woman with a yoga mat under one arm and a Nalgene bottle in her hand.

"She's just getting changed, but you can set up." Kathy's voice disappears down the hall.

Under his breath, Jack mutters, "And we've been dismissed. For *yoga*."

* * * *

"So. Lynn Baldwin." Jack uses his chopsticks to push a slice of dragon roll across the platter towards me. "What's your first impression?"

We've had more than a few lunch meetings at Mikado. It's a mediocre sushi place sandwiched between a mediocre boutique and a revolving-tenant space that has been a pet grooming salon, a Pilates studio, and, very briefly, an oxygen bar. No one comes here to make deals, be seen, or listen in.

I take a long breath through my nose as I consider. Jack values honesty, but my position is difficult. Lynn Baldwin is a guaranteed money-maker, the perfect white soccer mom living the American dream and sexually empowering other women. Since I'm asking to be a part of that, it's probably not a good idea to tell Jack that while Lynn comes across as perfectly harmless—friendly, even—there's something about her that rubs me the wrong way. I chalk it up to professional jealousy and remind myself of the mental vow I made less than an hour ago.

"She's enthusiastic. She clearly wants this project to succeed."

Jack pours himself more hot tea. "Why wouldn't she?"

"I don't know. Maybe I was expecting someone difficult." I shrug.

"Oh, she can be difficult," he warns. "You should have seen some of the back and forth we had negotiating for the rights."

"Too many creative demands?" I ask, my anxiety soaring.

"That, and the money." Jack tilts his head to the side with a half-grimace.

"Her agent handled that, didn't he?" Baldwin is represented by a huge, prestigious firm. Any difficulty Macrocosm had on the financial front probably came from them. Lynn Baldwin the person might have set off some alarm bells in my head, but Lynn Baldwin the female writer deserves some defending.

"He did."

"So, she wants you to pay to share some of her success. Why's that a problem? Dan Brown sold the rights to *The Da Vinci Code* for six million dollars. I didn't hear anyone complaining about *that*." I fix Jack with a look that dares him to argue back.

"You didn't hear anything back then," he points out cheerfully. "You were still doing improv workshops."

"I have never done an improv workshop." He damn well knows what I was doing back then, but he's never thrown it in my face, and I wouldn't let him, anyway. "The last thing in the world I would ever want to be is an actress."

"Good. You're a better writer than you are a liar. You didn't care for Ms. Baldwin, either."

He has me there.

"I don't have to like someone to defend them from shitty, misogynist attitudes. And you need to examine yours." For added spite, I eat the last piece of tuna sashimi.

"All I'm saying is that she's not peaches and cream and sunshine. She wants so much control, she might as well do the movie on her own. And she already wants to talk casting. She's got her eye on one actor and one alone."

"Which actor?" I have a feeling I won't be surprised.

"Jason McEwan."

Nope, not surprised at all. McEwan is the hottest young star in Hollywood, at the moment, fresh off a series of teen werewolf movies. "Aren't you disappointed that it's not you?"

"I can't play twenty-nine, anymore." That's bullshit, because Jack knows that for men, forty is Hollywood thirty. "Not that it isn't flattering knowing I was the inspiration."

How Jack fits his ego through doors, I'll never know.

After lunch, I head home invigorated by the promise of a new project. It's been a long time since I've been able to get really, truly excited over something. To a writer, there's nothing more satisfying than the sound of busy fingers on a keyboard. I haven't heard that in a long time. Since I finished the screenplay for my last film, I've had writer's block of epic proportions. Because of this, I'm going to be grateful, graceful, and committed to this script.

If I don't, I'll never get through it.

I pull up to the gate at my apartment complex and swipe my card. The driveway pulls a tight circle around a stone fountain situated on an island of terra cotta brick. The buildings are newish, only just built in 2004, but it was designed with what the realtor described as "the flavor of Spanish mission style, with an art deco spin". In other words, a new building they tried to make look old. I pull my car beneath the wide arch of the parking garage entrance and into my space. My apartment is on the ground floor, across a rectangular courtyard with another fountain.

The moment I get through the door, my clothes come off. My jacket is already gone; I tossed it into the backseat after my lunch with Jack. I leave my clothes like a trail of breadcrumbs through the apartment, all the way to my closet, where I change into cut-off sweats and a tank top.

I wasn't throwing out empty protestations when I told Jack that I don't want to be an actress. That's bullshit that every woman in L.A. gets accused of, regardless of her true aspirations. But writing has always been my passion, and that's due in part to the fact that I don't have to get up in the middle of the night to let someone slather makeup all over my face and force me into uncomfortable clothes. I respect the women who do it—without them, I wouldn't have a job—but there but for the grace of God.

And—not to give myself too much credit—that's never going to change unless writers change it. For every blond bombshell with pale skin, blue eyes, and heels so high she risks breaking her ankles, I write two dark-skinned women with PhDs and natural hair. For every manic pixie dream girl who helps a twenty-something white guy find his way off Zoloft, I write two women who fix their own lives while taking their damn meds.

The problem is, none of that sells a movie. Those are the kinds of characters that live in novels. If they do make it to the screen, their flaws are smoothed out. A paunchy, unlikeable alcoholic on a train becomes Emily Blunt with perfect cheekbones and an air of vulnerability the audience can digest.

In a perfect world, I would be able to smoothly transition into writing books without sacrificing my financial security, but I don't live in a perfect world, and the bills I have stacked on my desk are very, very real. So, I sit down, turn on my Mac, and ignore the accusing presence of my unfinished novel in its lonely Scrivener window.

*I'll finish you. Someday. I promise.*

For now, I've got another person's novel to concentrate on. I prop my annotated copy of *Beautiful Darkness* on a stand beside my keyboard, open to the first chapter.

*Standing in front of my mirror, I take in my reflection. Dull brown hair that my best friend, Caroline, often refers to as "mousy". Eyes that are far too big and unnervingly blue in my face.*

"Where the hell else are you going to keep your eyes?" I ask the narrator aloud.

*My body is too slender. I often wish that I had been born in the 1920's, when a lean, size two body was the standard of feminine beauty.*

I roll my eyes and scan the rest of the page. Paragraph upon paragraph of the heroine delivering a humble-brag monologue about her milk-pale skin, perky breasts that sadly negate her need to buy sexy bras, and how her high cheekbones give her a "*haughty air*".

The story doesn't actually begin until the bottom of page two.

*"I can't believe you're picking work over a trip to Vale." Caroline, my best friend and roommate, stands behind me, twisting a lock of her perfectly curled blond hair around one finger. Caroline is attractive, in a boring, conventional way. Her skin is bronzed from the many hours she spends surfing. It must be nice to have rich parents who can indulge your every whim. At least she has a friend like me, who doesn't judge her for her lazy lifestyle. Most people from my modest background would be jealous of someone who doesn't have to work.*

*"I have to." I remind her. "I need to pay my half of the rent. And this is my first post-college job. I have to build my résumé."*

I tap my fingers lightly on my keyboard. I obviously can't begin a screenplay with the heroine standing in front of a mirror, thinking about how hot she is. I decide to skip ahead, to the actual beginning.

*FADE IN:*

*EXT. LOS ANGELES SKYLINE – DAY*
*The opening credits roll over shots of the city. Not just the glamor and glitz, but the dirt and the grit. A juxtaposition of everything DAMIAN BENNET stands for, and everything he truly is. Interspersed with these shots, we see the man himself. Not his face. Not yet. His collection of fine suits. His fingers drifting over the keys of a piano. The scars on his knuckles from too many fights.*

God, I've made him sound like the Phantom of the Opera. I can fix that later.

*CUT TO:*

*INT. OFFICE BUILDING – DAY*

*A pale young brunette woman sits in a cubicle in a hectic bullpen. She bites her lip as she stares intently at a computer screen. The woman is ELLA VAUGHN. She's 22 and working her first post-college job as a reporter for the L.A. Herald.*
*A man approaches her cubicle and leans against it. He is JACKSON FOSCO. He is in his mid- to late-30's, tall and rail thin. He exudes an oily, intimidating*

I pause. How do I describe this man without writing, "telegraphs as the clear villain of the piece?"

*He exudes an oily, intimidating presence that would repel women in the workplace.*

> *JACKSON*
> *Ella. How are you settling in?*

> *ELLA*

*Very well, thank you. Everyone here is so patient. Whenever I have a question, someone—*

JACKSON
*That's great, that's great. I have an assignment for you.*

*Jackson enters the cubicle, getting too close for comfort.*

JACKSON
*Have you heard of underground fighting?*

It's easy to lose track of time when I'm writing. Phone alarms are the only thing standing between me and starvation, most days. My phone chirps at seven, but tonight, it's not reminding me about dinner. I abandon my work and grab a sandwich, but food is the furthest thing from my mind.

I have a very important meeting tonight.

There's a reason my office doesn't get its own room in my two-bedroom apartment. The other room is just mine, for special occasions. I flip on the light. Far from the luxurious BDSM dungeon in *Beautiful Darkness*, mine is modest, but not shabby. It's close quarters, but there's still room for a multi-purpose bench for spanking and bondage—a modified adjustable spa table with tie down rings—a wooden chair with leather straps on the arms, and a big cabinet stocked with lots and lots of really fun toys. I'd been building my collection since I'd first learned about BDSM in college. It's evolved over the years to include body-safe toys and higher quality floggers, paddles, and restraints. The furniture definitely had to wait until I could afford to live without roommates. Now that I have it, this second bedroom is a sanctuary. And only one person has ever been in it, besides me.

I kneel beside the table and slide open the panel door of the built-in storage cupboard. There's a gallon bottle of water-based lube with a pump top, and I take it with me to my bedroom. My favorite latex dress hangs in the back of the

21

closet. I remove the garment carefully and lay it across my bed. Then, I strip down and pump the lube into my hands.

Putting on my outfit is one of my favorite parts of my pre-scene ritual. Latex is a lot of work to get on, but it's easier since I switched from powder to lube. I smear it all over the inside of the dress and untie the high collar, then wriggle into the more-than-skin-tight suit. Once every wrinkle is carefully smoothed down and I feel like I can move without ripping the extremely fragile material, I slide on some black thigh-highs with a back seam. Fishnets are too obvious a choice, in my opinion. I fasten the stockings to the garter clips on the hem of the dress and turn to my mirror to tie up the sweet black bow at the neck. Then, I check myself out.

The midnight black latex hugs my body from just barely under the curve of my ass, all the way up to my neck. The short sleeves are slightly puffed, and a heart-shaped keyhole frames my cleavage. I do a celebratory wiggle. When I had first started dressing for scenes, I felt silly, like a kid playing dress up. With some practice, getting suited up and ready made me feel powerful. After a while, it became a uniform. Once it's on, I'm on the job.

I scrape my dark hair up into a high ponytail on top of my head and freshen my makeup, exaggerating my cat-eye liner a little more, and contouring my cheekbones a little sharper.

My doorbell rings. I don't rush to get it. Instead, I find my black leather stiletto pumps with the rounded toes and slip them on. Then, I saunter to the living room and wait.

He has a key. The bell just announces his arrival. The lock clicks, and the doorknob turns. I take a deep breath, anticipation setting every nerve in my body on fire.

The door opens, and Jack steps inside.

December 23, 2004

"Did you hear who's out there?" Teresa—"Starla" on stage—asks, grabbing my hand and nearly causing me to drag my eyeliner across my cheek.

I jerk my hand away. "The drunkest men in L.A.?"

"The drunkest and the richest," she confirms, but goes on, "Seriously, guess who's having his bachelor party in the VIP section *tonight*."

"I don't keep up on celebrity gossip." At least, not celebrity wedding gossip. I constantly read all the industry gossip. If I have no idea who's working where and on what, I can't realistically expect to break in.

"Just ask me who's out there!" Teresa pleads.

"Fine. Who's out there?"

Her eyes flare wide. "Jack. Martin."

Celebrities come into the club all the time. After a while, dancers just get used to it. We've all given private dances to men who wear watches that cost twice our annual earnings. But every now and then, just the right someone could come in and make you star struck.

"Wow." A celebrity bachelor party is a gold mine. They drop tons of cash in tips and dances just so the tab gets splashed across the tabloid sites the next day.

Teresa goes to her locker and pulls out her makeup case. She leans into the mirror and reapplies her lipstick. "I swear to God, I better get some of their money. I'm not kidding. Tuition went up this fall."

I shake my head and laugh to myself. The money would be awesome, but I'm not sure how I feel about dancing in front of someone I've sexually fantasized about before.

Of course, I kind of do that every day. I've had a lot of good times thinking of my co-workers while I shower. Including Teresa.

There's a knock on the door in warning, and Brenda pops her head in. She's a short woman in her sixties, with curly gray hair and a perpetually pissed-off look on her face. "Hey. Shift's started, ladies. I got two empty stages, and I'm just itching to fine someone."

I push my chair back. "Yes, dear."

Brenda's panic about empty stages is ridiculous, but that's Brenda. The fact that it's a Thursday before a major holiday has resulted in a packed club. The soft blue light on the walls reflects off my shimmery silver dance bottoms as I cross the floor. When I first started dancing, it seemed weird to just strut out half-naked. Now, I'm surprised I don't accidentally stroll into the post office topless. I try to keep my eye out for a spot near the VIP section. Like a beautiful miracle, Ben, the D.J., switches up songs and announces, "Heading to the Crystal stage, it's the always lovely Jasmine. And next up on the main stage, we've got a little Caribbean spice for y'all. Please welcome Miss Starla!"

The crystal stage was named so because of its folded mirror background. It's smaller than the main stage, but it's so close to the VIP section, you can almost taste the criminally overpriced Grey Goose. I am so going to tip Ben big time at the end of the night.

The smaller stages dance to whatever the main stage girl likes. Right now, that's "Turn Me On" by Kevin Little, so I'm not complaining. It has a good rhythm and a sensual beat. I go through a few moves causally, paying more attention to the guys at the foot of the stage than the ones in the VIP section. I don't want to hold out for a big catch and let the smaller ones go.

I swing around the pole with one hand, then slide it up, stretching myself out for a few sinuous body waves. And that's when I see him.

He's seated in the middle of a round banquette, and the dim lighting from the overhead fixture casts his face into mostly shadow. But I know it's him; everybody in America would probably recognize him. I also know that, if I could see his eyes, they would be locked on me. So, I smile my most practiced come-and-get-me smile and swing playfully around the pole again.

Then, I remember there are men at the rail, money in hand. Men at my feet, begging for my attention. That's the part of this job that I really enjoy. It's hard to separate my kink from my job, when so much of my job is based on other people's kinks. Some of them would crawl for me if I asked them to, and they would pay to do it.

Instead, I crawl for them, slowly, tossing my hair, taking their money with my teeth or my tits. The shy gentlemen toss it directly on the stage. But even while I'm occupied with them, I feel one particular set of eyes on me.

When the song ends, and I come down, one of the waitresses is waiting for me.

"A gentlemen in the VIP section wants to buy you a drink."

My heart pounds so hard in my chest, I feel like I'm going to throw up. I try not to think of the many ways this could be a meet-cute in a screenplay, because I would rather die than let on to one of the most powerful actors in Hollywood that I'm an aspiring screenwriter. I don't want to be *that* person, the one who pitches in elevators or slides scripts under bathroom stalls.

The waitress leads me to the party. It's a group of about thirty guys, all at various stages of intoxication, spread out over all six banquettes. There are already girls dancing on the low mirrored tables. On all of them except one. That's where we stop, directly in front of Jack Martin.

"Hey, there she is." A sweaty white kid with a backwards trucker hat points at me. I'm almost a hundred percent sure I've seen him on a TV sitcom. "Jack, my dog, you have to do it, now. We got her over here."

Like getting me to come over is some big accomplishment. I fix my attention on Jack. "I hear this is your bachelor party. Congratulations."

"This man—" Trucker Hat holds back a burp or a barf, I don't want to know which. "—needs a lap dance."

"Is that right?" I put one hand on my hip, and with the other, I slowly crook a finger at Jack Martin. "Let's go somewhere more private."

He grimaces apologetically. "My friend here has good intentions, but I'm not—"

"Don't be such a fucking pussy." Trucker Hat shoves what amounts to my next month's rent at me, and Jack Martin groans in surrender. He stands and pushes his way past the other friends in the banquette, nearly falling across the table.

Okay, so, he's had a few.

"I'm about to be a married man, dude," he complains to Trucker Hat, who laughs and makes a face.

"No sex in the champagne room. Chris Rock said so." Then, he makes a big, exaggerated wink at me that makes me want to gag. Of course, sweaty guys in ironic trucker hats think we're selling sex in the back rooms. If they had any idea how many girls I'd seen fired for trying that shit in the past year...

"Chris Rock is a wise man," I tell them, trying to be flirty with my warning. "The bouncer is going to have similar instructions for you."

Jack Martin's eyes rake up and down my body. "Well, I am prepared to follow any instructions necessary."

"You take good direction," I quip, and he actually grins at that.

Of course, it's not hard to impress drunk guys with your wit when you're standing there topless.

I take his hand and pull him with me toward the padded swinging door at the back. The VIP section has two private rooms of its own. Through the door is one of our bouncers, and while he gives my movie star customer the rules, I hastily straighten the bills in my hand and fix them to the ankle-strap of my shoe with a rubber band.

"Purple one's open," the bouncer says with a nod toward me. He's new. I think his name is Rick. It's hard to keep track, sometimes. We have a high turnover rate when it comes to security and wait staff.

The purple room, like the crystal stage, has a pretty unimaginative named inspired by the purple walls, carpet, and violet side-lighting. I lead Jack Martin in, and he takes a seat on the purple padded bench.

"Look," he says as I stand in front of him. "My friend out there, he's a douche bag."

"But he's still your friend?" I sway to the music and rake my hair back through my fingers. The song is more than halfway over, so I won't count this toward his dance.

"How much money did he give you?" Jack Martin asks. I can't stop thinking of him with his whole name. He's not just a customer. He's a major movie star, and I'm standing in front of him, topless.

But in a place like this, that's sometimes all you need to bring a man completely to his knees. Sometimes, literally.

One of the most powerful stars in Hollywood? He would be the ultimate challenge.

In answer to his question, I shrug and turn, bending over so he gets an up-close and personal view of my ass in my very tiny heart-backed g-string. I flick through the bills fastened to my ankle and look back at him. "Enough for a couple dances and a two-hundred percent tip."

He shakes his head, eyes downcast like he's embarrassed. "Fair enough. I just want to know how long I can hide in here before I have to go back out to—"

He waves an arm at the door.

"Ah." There are the guys who get private dances because they want a naked woman to grind on them, and there are the guys who get them just to have someone to talk to. Then, there are the guys who come to a private room to save face in front of their friends. That requires a totally different tactic. I straighten and pretend to let my persona slip a little. "You're not really here for a dance, are you?"

"You can keep the money," he says quickly. "I'm not asking about that."

"No, I get it." I motion to the spot beside him. "You mind if I..."

"No, please." He scoots over and gestures for me to sit down. "Those heels look like real killers."

"They're not great," I admit. To keep us from lapsing into awkward silence, I ask, "So, not into exotic dancers?"

"It's nothing personal. It's just, I'm getting married in two days. Seems wrong." He shrugs.

"You're not one of those guys who sees their bachelor party as their last night of 'freedom'?" I snort before I can help myself. Most men that come into the club don't like being laughed at.

He leans back, shaking his head. "If I was worried about losing my freedom, I wouldn't be getting married."

"See, I respect that," I say, because I really do. "We get some patrons in here that want to bang a stripper on their last night in the wild, like it's not cheating if they do it before this arbitrary deadline."

Shit. I shouldn't talk bad about men while I'm on the job, no matter how sympathetic a client seems.

But Jack Martin is cool with it. He even agrees with me, judging from relieved roll of his eyes and the hand he holds up like he's testifying in church. "Thank you. You know, the guys out there...they're not my friends. They can be all right, but it's mostly industry people. You don't like hanging out with people you work with after you go home, right?"

"You've got me there." I don't tell him that I don't really hang out with anyone. I only moved to L.A. the year before, and it takes me a long time to get close to people. The most socializing I do is call my sister in the mornings and fill her in on the details of my crazy late-night shift at the imaginary diner I imaginary waitress at.

"I don't even know why I'm telling you all of this," he says, dropping his head in embarrassment. "I'm supposed to be back here watching you shake it."

"Well, I can still 'shake it'," I tease, making air quotes with my fingers. "Some people find it easier saying stuff to a stranger. You're never going to see me again, so it's safe."

"Safe, until you run to a tabloid." The drunken bitterness in his voice startles me. He seems nice, but a lot of guys seem nice. Is he going to flip out and threaten me not to breathe a word to anyone or else?

"I'm not going to run to a tabloid," I promise.

But he's drunk, and I've already been convicted. "Yeah, right. You'll see if you can get a better paycheck out of me, first."

What a fucking asshole. I guess I should have anticipated this. The guys out there in the VIP section might not be his friends, but they're still here with him. He might be more like them than he gives himself credit for.

Without thinking, I snap, "Right, because I don't have any aspirations in life beside stealing men's money."

He looks instantly chastened, which is a relief, because it means we're probably not going to get into a situation where the bouncer has to come in. "Sorry. I'm sorry. I'm really drunk, and I'm saying a lot of stuff that I shouldn't."

"Yeah." I think about all the money I've already made, and all the money that's still out there to be made. If I get up and leave, now, his friend is going to complain to the management. So, I just sit there, waiting for Jack Martin, movie star and drunken dickweed, to decide the course of the rest of the song.

After an uncomfortably long silence, he asks, "So, what are they?"

"What are what?" I cross my arms over my chest.

"Your aspirations."

It's easier for me to be naked in front of someone than to have an earnest conversation with them. I don't know how to proceed.

"Let me guess. You want to be an actress," he says, without a hint of judgment.

I shake my head. "Nope."

"Law school?" he guesses. "Nursing school—no, medical school! That's it, isn't it? You want to be a doctor."

"I would make a terrible doctor." I catch sight of myself in one of the mirrors. Me, sitting next to Jack Martin. It was probably as close to my dream of working in Hollywood as I would ever get.

When you meet someone famous, they seem wrong, somehow. You've got an image in your head of how they're going to be and who they are. Finding out they're real people makes them seem less real. Meeting Jack Martin, being so close to someone with his level of success, makes my dream seem less real, too.

"So? I make a terrible actor." He flashes me the smile that got him named *People*'s Sexiest Man Alive a year ago. "Seriously, though. If this isn't your career, what do you want to do?"

I don't know why I feel such a burning need to say it. The last thing I want is for him to think I'm fishing. I've got too much pride for that. I could make something up and not sound sleazy and grasping. But I don't hold it back. I just pray that he doesn't laugh.

"I want to be a screenwriter."

## Chapter Two

Standing in the small foyer of my apartment, Jack bows his head. "Mistress."

"You're late. Four minutes late." In this role, I don't do pleasantries.

"I apologize, Mistress." He keeps his gaze cast to the floor.

"And you're unprepared. You haven't even undressed, yet." If I had my riding crop, I could smack it against my palm. Missed opportunity. "Take off your clothes. I'm watching the clock."

His tie is already loosened. He pulls it over his head and unbuttons his shirt. The cuffs are undone. He kicks off his shoes as he works his belt buckle. And I wait. His scramble to disrobe might seem comical to an outsider, but his increasingly frantic movements get my blood pumping. Every fumble of his fingers, every agitated breath at his own excited clumsiness is proof of how much he wants to please me. How quickly he wants me to assume even more power over him.

"Four minutes late," I repeat, clucking my tongue. "That's four plus what you earned last time."

Four more edges plus the five he already had coming to him. I don't think he's ever waited out nine before. He doesn't look happy at the prospect, though we both know that extra teasing only makes the outcome better.

He doesn't reply to me, because I haven't asked him a question. He knows better than to speak without permission.

When he's naked, I let my eyes wander over him. Los Angeles doesn't suffer from a lack of personal trainers, and Jack's body is ample proof of that. Back home in Nebraska, guys in their forties don't generally look like Jack. Hell, most places in the world guys in their *thirties* don't look like Jack. The muscles of his arms are big and well-defined. Without a shirt on, the thickness of his neck is more apparent. His calves and thighs are so round and perfect that I want to bite them—and I often do. His pecs are tight and square, his abs ridiculously defined, and a v-shaped Adonis Belt of muscle leads the eye right down to an absolutely gorgeous cock. It's long, but not too long, when erect—which he's very quickly becoming under my scrutiny—with a slight upward curve that could have been designed by a sex toy company and thickness I could almost get my thumb and forefinger around.

Almost.

Hot blood rushes to my face at the memory of Jack, cock in his hand as he pulled out of me and jerked himself off the rest of the way, while I leaned back on his desk, legs spread, thighs trembling.

That had been Jack and Jessica doing something impulsive and dangerous. That had been Jack, Jessica's boss, holding just a little bit more power than usual. That had been Jessica, already under Jack's command, letting him have yet another little piece of her.

Nope. Never again.

Jack and Jessica aren't in my apartment tonight. Just a sadistic mistress and her nameless submissive.

I snap my fingers. "Follow me."

He gets down on all fours, without my asking, and crawls behind me. With every step, liquid heat loosens my hips and thighs. This man, physically and charismatically powerful, *crawls* for me.

My props are already laid out: the bottle of lube, some paintbrushes, a feather, a vibrating probe. Some nights, he wants to be flogged or paddled. Some nights, he wants to go even harder.

Tonight, he's looking for flat-out torture.

"Stand up," I tell him. "Get on the bench."

"How would you like me, Mistress?" He cautiously lifts his gaze, and I narrow mine. He quickly looks down again.

"On your back. Put your hands by your side." I reach for my gloves, long, impersonal black latex that reaches to my elbows.

He positions himself obediently in the center of the table, hands at his sides, fingers flexing in anticipation.

I stand over him and inspect him from top to bottom with my arms folded over my chest. My tits push together more with the motion, and I see his throat move as he swallows.

"Here are my plans for tonight," I tell him, though we've already outlined the scene in an email. "I'm going to tickle you until you beg me to stop. I'm going to edge you until you weep. And then, I'm going to milk every last drop out of you."

He closes his eyes. "Oh, yes, please, Mistress."

My pussy aches. By the end of the night, his denial will be my denial. His torment will be my torment.

At the moment, his is just a little more direct. I select two pairs of padded leather cuffs from the wall and slip one set around his wrists. They chain to the loops around the table, but they don't allow for much give. Just enough that he can maintain a comfortable position.

"Over your head," I murmur, sliding my gloved hand up his arm. A shudder runs through him.

I fasten the cuffs to the ring at the head of the table then I take the other pair of restraints and slip them around his ankles. For now, I leave his legs free.

Just restraining him is enough to get him painfully hard. His cock twitches against his stomach, the tight pink head peeking out from his foreskin. I run my hands up the insides of his legs, my fingertips almost grazing his balls before I pull away.

He's breathing heavy.

He's going to have a long night.

I select the feather from my arsenal and draw the tip across my bottom lip as I approach him. Hunger and fear war in his expression, and I smile cruelly down at him. "You're terrified."

"Yes, Mistress." That's what he likes. The fear, the helplessness. Jack is a man who's never helpless. He's always guarded, always in charge. The only time he ever relinquishes control is under my hands, and that makes me feel powerful in a way nothing else does.

I start at his forehead, right at the hairline, and swoop the feather down the center of his nose. He tilts his head back, seeking more contact. I roll the tip of the feather along his jaw. His breath speeds up as I approach his ear. There's a ticklish spot right behind it. I take my time getting there, stroking the outer rim of his ear before I home in on the sensitive spot. It's not as bad as his sides or armpits or the soles of his feet, but it still makes him squirm.

"Do you know what I like best about this?" I ask, leaning close to his ear. "I like that you know it's going to get worse. And I love how much you hate wanting it."

I sweep the edge of the feather down his arm, from wrist to armpit, and he jerks at the restraints out of pure reflex, gasping. I swirl it in that hollow, teasing over the hair. His body tightens, and he wriggles, his natural instinct to lower his arm prevented by the cuffs.

You can only tickle one spot for just so long before the nerves stop responding. Before that can happen, I draw loops over his chest, circling his nipples along the way. They're flat and brown and hard, and so, so sensitive. He gasps and rocks his hips as much as he can; a drop of precum already leaks from his cock.

If he can make it through three edges tonight, I'll be surprised.

I tease him with the feather, making lazy swirls over his shoulder and upper arm, straying closer and closer to his armpit, and I'm pleased to get the same reaction out of him as from the other side. This time, he can't help his reflexive giggle.

I slap him across the face, the latex glove creating a loud crack that makes the strike sound ten times worse than it was.

"I'm sorry, Mistress!" he shouts in a panic, before I can hit him again.

"Keep your filthy mouth shut, or I'll shut it for you." I have a really great gag shaped like the head of a penis; I don't know why the idea of stuffing a cock in Jack's mouth gets me off. It just does.

Watching him struggle not to laugh as I move from using the feather to using my hands is almost as good as watching him try to hump the air when I pick up the feather again and drag it down his chest. I bring the tip of the feather down, down, over his wildly contracting abs, circling his belly button, stopping just short of what he really wants me to touch.

Instead, I tease his inner thighs, the backs of his knees, down to his pedicured feet—Jack is vain from head-to-toe, literally. I lightly rake my nails along one instep, and he twists his foot back and forth. There's nowhere to run. He's practically screaming behind his closed lips.

And I'm just getting started.

I toss the feather aside and reach for one of the paintbrushes. It's brand new, flat, and silky soft. I paint it dry up the arch of one of his feet. He jerks reflexively back, so I know it's time for the ankle restraints. After I lock him down, I pump the lube into my hand, dip the brush, and tease the sole of that foot again.

"Oh, god," he whimpers, all of his toes flexing and curling.

"What did I say about that gag?" I ask.

He squeezes his eyes shut. "May I have permission to speak, Mistress?"

I tilt my head, considering. "All right. You may speak."

"You're driving me crazy." His agonized voice breaks as I slide the bristles of the oily brush between two of his toes.

"Good. Then, I'm doing what you came here for."

I'm a patient person. Jack is not. So, luckily, he's the one tied up. He curses under his breath as I slowly paint the liquid over one foot, then the next, with aching slowness. I hum to myself a little, so absorbed in my task that, for a moment, I forget that the parts I'm teasing belong to a person.

A person grinding his teeth so hard they squeak.

I laugh. "You're so pathetic."

"I'm sorry, Mistress," he gasps.

"I'm not." I continue with the brush and the lube, up to his ankle. "I love that you're this weak. I love that you're going to beg me to let you come. And I love that you're going to beg me to stop."

"Oh, god." His Adam's apple bobs as he swallows.

I take an excruciating amount of time to work up his legs. When I reach his groin, he's so hard it looks painful. I dip the brush again and barely glide it across his scrotum, pulled tight to his body. He groans, and his cock leaps, a long string of precum stretching between the head and his stomach.

I stop a moment to lean close to his ear. "You want me to touch it, don't you?"

"Yes, Mistress." His throat sounds painfully dry. "Yes, god, please."

Standing, I shrug. "No."

My denial makes him fight the restraints, just for a second. He knows disobedience will be punished. It only takes a single look from me to quiet him.

"You're already getting nine tonight. I can't image you'd want to add more."

His eyes go wide with fear.

"Do you want me to add more?" I ask him.

"No! No, Mistress. I don't want to add more." There was that begging I was so looking forward to.

There are certain things he has no control over, so of course I'm not going to penalize him for his cock bobbing around. And I'm sure he knows that, but probably not in the state he's in.

I spread the lube all over him, drizzling it up his torso and distributing it with maddeningly precise flicks of the paintbrush. His hands are fists above his head. I skip nothing;

even his shoulders and arms glisten by the time I'm done. The only thing I haven't touched is his cock, and he moans in anticipation as I smooth my gloved hands down his body toward it.

Then, I draw them away and pick up the other paintbrush I've saved for just this moment. The bristles are long and come to an incredibly fine point. It won't provide anywhere near the level of stimulation he's hoping for. When he sees it, he groans.

"I didn't ask for your opinion." I dip the brush into some of the lubricant and hover it over the shaft of his penis. He lifts his head as much as he can to try to see what I'm doing. When I'm sure he has a good view, I slowly lower the point of the brush until it's just barely out of reach of his leaping cock.

I go back to his feet.

"No! No, please! Please!"

There it is.

I laugh at him and smack the bottoms of his feet, hard. He hisses in pain.

I go back to his cock and slowly drag the tip of the brush up the seam between his balls, diverting to follow the path of the one of the distended veins on his shaft. There is no way such a touch could possibly satisfy him. I take some lube in my gloved palms and drizzle it down the center of his cock. I still haven't touched it with my hands, and he's going mad.

The thing is, it's not all about the torture. Sure, it's fun to watch him struggling and begging and fighting for control. But the anticipation is good, too. Knowing that by taking my time, by teasing him until he forgets where he is, forgets a life that exists outside of the searing need, he will experience pleasure so intense that it overwhelms all of his senses...that's a big part of what gets me off.

Just not with him. That's the line we don't cross, anymore.

I draw loops up the underside of his shaft with the brush and lube, all the way to where the head peeks out from the foreskin. I trace around the edge and gently work the bristles under that band of skin. His hips jerk up. I don't need to add any more lube; I glide my brush through the bead of precum poised at his tip and pull it backwards in a line, letting the point of the bristles dip into his urethra just a bit. He hisses and writhes in discomfort.

"You don't like that?" I ask, and do it again, back and forth over the slit. "Tell me what you would like."

"Touch me, Mistress," he begs. "Please!"

I toss the paintbrush aside and pump more of the lube into my hands. When I rub them together above his cock, the liquid slides easily away from my latex-covered palms. Lube runs over his hips to puddle on the bench beneath him. Then, slowly, before his pleading eyes, I take hold of him in both of my hands and glide my palms down the sides of his shaft.

I can almost taste his moan on my tongue.

His cock is so hard, I can't help but imagine it inside me. And it's easy to imagine. It's been inside me before. My pussy clenches in hungry need, and it takes me a moment to redirect my thoughts.

I concentrate on my hands, pulling one fist up his length, followed by the other in a long, endless stroke. He tries to pump against my hand, and I release him, letting his cock slap wetly against his stomach.

His "No, no, no!" isn't directed at me, but at his fragile will.

So, I take pity on him, this time, and go back to work. It's easy to get lost in the rhythm. It can be downright hypnotic. But I have to pay attention to his body's cues; he's not going to orgasm until I say so tonight. He's just going to come damn close.

"Remember, you have to tell me if you're going to come," I remind him. "Or what happens?"

Through gritted teeth, he groans, "Chastity for a week."

"A whole week of no touching. No release." I rub my thumb over his sensitive tip, and his body jerks. I smile to myself. "And you don't want me to ruin that last orgasm you do have."

He clamps his lips tight. His balls draw up. I cup them and tug them down, and he shouts, "I'm close!"

Releasing him, I turn to my assorted goodies. "That's one. Bring your arousal down. Let me know when I can touch you, again."

I select the triple ring and stretch it out. If it were a more rigid material, I would have to start with his penis flaccid, but the gummy ring has plenty of flexibility. I wait until he gives me the all clear and slide the first ring down his shaft. Then, I lift his balls and stretch the remaining rings over them, forcing them down and apart. When he comes, the resistance will make it that much more intense.

"Time out," he says. "Are you really going to go for nine edges tonight? Because it might take longer than I should wear this thing."

"You couldn't make it through six edges tonight," I tell him. "No, I'll probably go for five."

He nods as much as he can in his position, clearly relieved. "Okay. Time in."

When I first started out as a Dom, a split-second break like that could shake my entire mindset. Now, I recognize it as a necessary part of that mindset; a Dom who can't check in on their sub can't properly protect their sub.

I close my fist around him, again, and pump slowly, until he strains and swears and begs me to stop because I've brought him too close. It's only through sheer determination that he doesn't come all over his stomach.

The third edge is harder to reach, and once I get him there, I know I need reinforcements, and he needs a break from the repetitive stimulation. I take up the vibrating probe and inspect it as though I'm seeing it for the first time. I run my fingers around the girthy bulb and cluck my tongue. "This is much, much too big for your ass, isn't it?"

"Yes, Mistress." He's not just playing along; he's always exceptionally tight.

"Open your legs."

Even though his ankles are shackled down, he's got enough slack to let his knees fall open, leaving his ass vulnerable. I lube up my finger, and even with the slippery latex I can barely get it inside him. He hisses his discomfort, but he doesn't call me off. I stretch him as best as I can, until I can insert a second finger. I feel along the bottom of his passage, until my fingers encounter the bulb of his prostate. I press firmly, the way he likes it, and he moans.

"I could make you come like this," I tease.

"Oh, yes, Mistress. Yes, you could." He rocks his hips a little, but the way I've strapped him down doesn't allow for much movement. I withdraw my fingers and reach for the probe. "Are you ready for your favorite part?"

His eyes are already squeezed shut in anticipation of the pain. "Yes, Mistress."

I cup my hand and pump a ridiculous amount of lube into it. With my other hand, I spread his cheeks apart and swipe some of the liquid into the cleft of his ass. It's way more lubrication than strictly needed, but better too much than not enough. Especially considering how rough he likes it. Without any further warning, I push the slick bulbous end of the toy into him. Hard.

He lets out a sound between a groan and a shout of pain. I ignore him and push the toy into place. He exhales sharply from behind clenched teeth.

"There, there. Not so bad, was it?" I reach for his cock. Without the ring, it would have deflated a bit from the pain, but he's still rock hard and twitching. I hit the button on the probe, and it throbs to life inside him. He pumps his hips, thrusting his cock through my hand, and I meet each motion with a tight squeeze and lazy strokes.

He's almost there in mere seconds. I click off the probe before it can send him over.

"Oh, god, I have to come," he almost sobs.

"Only one more," I coo.

"Then, just fucking do it," he snaps.

"Excuse me?" I fix him with a sharp glare, and he swallows, his eyes going wide. I hit the button on the probe twice, ratcheting it up to the next setting. It's a steady pulse for four beats, followed by a long pause before the cycle starts over. He twists in a panic; he's had orgasms from just this toy before, and he knows I'll make good on my earlier threat.

"What was it?" I go on, lightly dragging one fingertip from the head of his cock all the way to the ring at the base. "If you come without permission, what will I do to you?"

"You'll…" He exhales heavily and tries again. Sweat stands out on his brow. "You'll ruin my orgasm. And then, I'll be in chastity for a week."

"And what's the penalty for talking to me the way you just did?" I rub the palm of my cupped hand over the head of his cock.

"You'll ruin the next one." He's been through that hell before; a week without touching himself, a week with no release, only to have it denied at the very last second. I love that punishment, letting go at the crucial moment, only to watch him frantically struggling for contact with anything as his cum slashes across his stomach, and his pleasure is snatched away.

"You don't want to do that, again, do you?" It's inevitable that, someday, he will; he likes the torture as much as I do.

He shakes his head. "No, Mistress. I'm sorry, Mistress."

The vibrator buzzes away in his ass, and his thighs contract and release with every buzz. I keep stroking him, picking up the pace a bit, until his twisting and panting give him away. Even before he warns me that he's about to come, I stop and cut off the probe. His hands are white-knuckled fists, his face is red.

"I don't understand why you want so badly to come." I lube up my hands, again. "You know you're just going to regret it after."

"Please," he begs, and I can't put him off any longer. It would just be cruel.

I turn the vibrations all the way up and jerk him off with fast, rough strokes. It doesn't take long; his toes are curling almost the instant I touch him. I increase my speed until my arm aches, and he bows up from the bench, straining toward the peak. By this time, his body is unsure of itself. He's been denied so long, it should seem impossible to him that he'll get any relief. All of his muscles tighten in a symphony of sinew and shadow accompanied by the keening song of his wail as he finally, *finally* comes, shooting rope after rope of cum all the way up to his chest.

"Look at the mess you made," I mock scold him. I scoop up some of the milky fluid with two fingers, then force them into his mouth. "Clean it up."

He sucks obediently on my gloved fingertips.

"Now, say thank you."

"Thank you, Mistress," he groans gratefully, his words garbled by my fingers in his mouth.

I'm still stroking him. His cock, trapped by the rings, stays hard, the thick vein on the underside throbbing visibly. I'll have to take the ring off soon; for now, though, it's doing exactly what it's meant to do.

I slide my hand up and down his shaft. His shivers of pleasure give way to shudders of discomfort. Strapped down, he has no way to defend himself. The panic in his eyes as he remembers that I'm not going to stop? That never gets old.

He pleads and begs, but he doesn't safe word, so I keep going.

"I don't understand what you're asking me for," I tease while he babbles incoherently. "Please faster? Is that what you're saying?"

"No! No!" His body jerks as I twist my hand around and around his raw red head, like I'm opening a particularly tough jar. The lube has absorbed into his skin, so there's not as much slip. It's rough, it's painful, and it elicits exactly the response I'm hoping for. He bucks and cries and whimpers, and I press the probe tighter against his prostate. His whole body lurches as though he'll topple the table.

I rub one finger around his urethra, through the cum that still dribbles from it. "I thought you were done, but I bet we can get more out. Should we?"

He's sobbing, now, and his neck cords as he tips his head back. His balls draw up, but the ring prevents them from going all the way. His head whips from side to side. "I can't, I can't—"

But he does. His toes flex, his back arches, and he cries out in agony as a few weak dribbles drip onto his stomach in the wake of his painful second orgasm.

"Enough!" Tears flow from the corners of his eyes and into his hair.

Now, I have to work fast. He rarely safe words; I've pushed him too far. I quickly stretch the triple ring and case everything out, trying not to touch him too much. I withdraw the probe and move on to the restraints.

"Almost done," I murmur, to keep him calm, as I unfasten him.

When he's free, he hesitantly lifts his arms. He rubs his wrists, staring blankly at the ceiling. His chest jerks with erratic breath. His eyes are red from his tears, and he shivers all over, totally depleted.

It's beautiful, and pitiful, the way he's come undone.

I take a box of baby wipes from beneath the bench and use them to gently clean his stomach and chest. I'm careful not to touch his overly sensitive penis; I give him a wipe to take care of that on his own.

His hands shake as he takes the moistened cloth, and I wait for him to finish up before I offer him my hand. "Let me help you."

He sits up but pauses for the head rush that follows. When he gets to his feet, I let him lean on me to walk him to the bathroom. The first thing he'll want is a shower. The second is some coffee.

"Are you okay?" I ask as he takes a towel from my tiny linen closet. "Do you want me to stay?"

He shakes his head. "Not this time. Go ahead. Put the coffee on?"

"Always."

I leave him and go to the kitchen, stripping off my gloves as I do. I wash my hands and set up the coffeepot. After I hit the brew button, I rinse my gloves in the sink, catching a glimpse of myself in the kitchen window. I have to laugh. It's too funny, the clash of the mundane domestic with profane kink.

A switch flips in my brain.

Any writer will attest that the moment inspiration strikes is also the moment that nothing can be done with that inspiration. I've got Jack in my shower, coming down from an intense scene. I've got a room that's going to need cleaning up. And I've been awake so long that I'm dead on my feet. I can't even think of writing until Jack is properly cared for.

I collect his clothes and take them to the bathroom, then duck into my room to wriggle carefully out of my latex. I grab my fluffy robe and wrap up, and when he emerges from the shower, I have his cup of coffee ready for him. He sits close to me on the couch, leaning his head on my shoulder. I don't rush him out; his aftercare is simple in comparison to some men I've been with, so I can't complain. Still, when his phone chirps, I'm not sorry that we're interrupted.

"Ask not for whom the Blackberry tolls," he says, sitting up and reluctantly sliding his half-empty mug onto the coffee table.

"I can't believe they still make those."

He reaches for the phone on the table. "Better security."

It doesn't surprise me that privacy is a concern for him. He has emotional walls thicker than a concrete bunker. The only time he ever lets them down is when I'm flat out torturing him. He should have joined the CIA, not become a movie star.

As we say our goodbyes, I'm already writing in the back of my mind.

"Thank you. It was great, as always." Jack gives me a lopsided smile. This is the only time I ever see him truly relaxed.

*It needs an aftercare scene.*

I nod and give him a brief hug. "Next Tuesday?"

"Next Tuesday," he confirms.

*She didn't include any aftercare scenes. That's why you never buy the romantic connection.*

He stops at the door and turns back to me. "When you have some pages—"

I hold up my hand. "I only discuss my projects with my boss, and I don't see him around here anywhere."

He nods. "Right. See you Tuesday."

It's not just Jack's boundaries I'm trying to protect. I need to keep my job separate for my own interests.

After he leaves, I clean up the room and all the toys we used, my brain flying at the speed of light. I've read *Beautiful Darkness*, I've studied it, but I've never connected to the romance. Now that I've realized exactly why that is, I worry that I'm going to have to veer further off course than I planned.

It's not rare for a movie to be different than the book it came from. Sure, people complain about it, but nobody really wanted to sit through every single page of *Harry Potter and the Half-Blood Prince*. Occasionally, a book can stay completely true to the novel. *Silence of the Lambs.* Scorsese's *The Age of Innocence.* But more often than not, something has to give.

I hope I can make *Beautiful Darkness* give without breaking it.

October 31, 2007

I secure my bag over my arm as I leave through the hotel lobby. I walk slowly, so the pleather I'm wearing doesn't squeak too much beneath my long wool coat. It doesn't really matter; Halloween is the one night of the year that my outfit won't raise too many eyebrows in the lobby of the Viceroy L'Ermitage. Still, after a night on the job, my emotions can be a little raw.

Consensually abusing a middle-aged guy who likes having cigarettes put out on his tongue can do that to a person.

I'm out the door and headed to my car when someone calls my name. Well, not my name. He yells, "Jasmine? Hey, Jasmine!"

Even though I haven't answered to my stage name in a long, long time, I turn out of reflex. Standing just beyond the door, a cigarette between his fingers, is Jack Martin.

He flicks the cigarette into the bushes and walks slowly toward me, his posture and movements casual and fluid. "What's a nice girl like you doing in a place like this?"

I'm too stunned that he's remembered me to actually answer him for a moment. Then, I stammer, "P-party."

It's what I tell everyone I'm doing if they recognize me at a hotel. I was at a party. But Jack Martin knows that I was a dancer, so he probably already assumes I was working the party, not attending it as a guest. I can't think of many of the girls from the club who just hang out at one of the most expensive hotels in the city.

His eyebrows lift, and he confirms my presumption. "You're working?"

"Um, yeah." I nod and look down at my stiletto-heeled patent leather boots. No need for him to know about my career upgrade. "We get fancy for Halloween."

"You should dress up like a cat." He pointed a finger gun at me. "Tail and everything. That would be hot."

"You're drunk." He was drunk the last time we met, too. I don't like drunk guys, but I also don't like to piss them off, so I soften my statement with, "You must be at a party, yourself."

"I am. A very boring party." His gaze skates up and down my body, and he frowns. "Is that part of the costume?"

"Oh, the coat?" I lift my arms. I'm starting to sweat under the pits. "Kind of."

He arches an eyebrow, giving his whole face that panty-melting bad boy look that he's practically trademarked.

That look is why I shrug back the shoulders of my coat, revealing the shiny straps of my black vinyl corset and the tons of cleavage mounded above it.

He leans back with a disbelieving, "Wow," and I feel more exposed than when I'd been standing practically naked in front of him in the V.I.P. room.

*Three years ago.*

The amount of time that's passed slaps me in the brain. I pull my coat back up, even though it's become torturously hot. "How were you able to remember me?"

"Really?" He laughs. "I don't want to be crude, but when a beautiful naked woman has a heart to heart with you on the worst night of your life, you tend to not forget her."

"The worst night of your... Oh." I remember too late what happened after that bachelor party. It was splashed all over the internet for weeks. Just hours before the wedding, his fiancé ran off. With Trucker Hat Guy. It was all anyone could talk about. I tuned most of it out, because I felt so damn bad for him, and also because several tabloids had written about his "tawdry" excursion to the club. Teresa told me to sell an interview, but as far as I was concerned, the V.I.P. room was a confessional that night. He didn't laugh at me when I told him I wanted to be a screenwriter, so I never breathed a word about the stuff he'd told me.

"Yeah, heard about that, did you?" He scratches his forehead with his thumb.

I wince in sympathy. "Everyone heard about that."

"That they did." He gives a grim laugh and a nod, but he can't look me in the face. "Hey, I just wanted to say thank you."

"For what?"

"For not running to the press, you know?" He looks up with a crooked smile. God, he's gorgeous. "A lot of people would have."

"Well, that would have been pretty sleazy of me, wouldn't it? I mean, right after you had your heart torn out in front of the whole world?" I wince. "Sorry."

"No, it's okay." He shakes his head. "I'm sorry, I shouldn't have bothered you. You were working."

"No, it's fine." But I can't stand on the sidewalk talking to him forever, and a few feet away, two young women stand huddled next to each other, chattering in excitement as they watch him. I smile at him. "It was cool catching up."

"Yeah. Yeah, it was." He opens his mouth as though he's going to say something. Then, he stops. "See ya."

"Bye." I turn around, trying to not to appear as awkward as I feel. Jack Martin seems like a pretty cool guy. Very genuine, if that night at the club was any indication. But famous men feel entitled to whatever woman they want. I had enough run-ins with that behavior in the club to know there was probably an ulterior motive for a guy like Jack Martin to make conversation with me.

After what happened with his fiancé and Trucker Hat Guy, maybe he's looking for another free therapy session.

I don't get far before he calls out, "Hey, Jasmine!"

When I turn, the two girls he's signing autographs for give me dark looks. I've interrupted their moment with a celebrity. I don't walk back.

"Yeah?"

"You still writing?" He hands a sharpie and one girl's phone back to her.

"Yeah." Not as much as I used to; the new job is mostly on-call and takes up more time than I'd ever anticipated.

"Excuse me for just one second. Stay right here," he tells the girls, and takes the sharpie back. They giggle as he jogs toward me.

He grabs my hand, and I pull back. But I don't pull entirely away, because his hand on mine feels better than any of the sex I've had in the past year. "What are you doing?"

"This," he says, uncapping the sharpie with his mouth, "is my email." He drags the tip of the marker across my skin. "My personal one, so I would appreciate it if it stayed between us."

"Okay." I frown down at my hand. How he managed to write so small and neat with a sharpie is some kind of witchcraft. "Why are giving it to me?"

"So, you can send me something. Pages, whatever you have finished." He caps the marker, again, and flashes a wide grin. "Or if you just want to keep in touch."

"Thanks." I have no idea if I'll do it or not. At the moment, I'm too stunned to think any further ahead than the breaths I'm taking.

"Okay, so…" He rocks back on his heels and gestures with his thumb at the girls still waiting behind him. "Have a good night, Jasmine."

Then, he turns and walks away, and I can't help myself. I call after him, "That's not my real name."

He doesn't look back. "I know."

## Chapter Three

"I don't understand. None of this in my book."

I sit across a conference table from Lynn Baldwin. Jack sits at her side, leafing through the pages I've completed over the past two weeks. The full script isn't ready, but Jack has succumbed to Lynn's constant barrage of emails begging to see something, anything.

Now, I feel like I'm on trial.

"I know," I tell her, trying hard not to sound apologetic. She might have a ridiculous amount of creative control, but I have persuasive arguments. "Film is a much different medium from a novel. While we're reading *Beautiful Darkness*, we're able to experience the romance through Ella's eyes. Almost as though we're Ella. Without the ability to be inside her head, though, we need a little more proof of what she sees in Damian."

"So, you just added a scene? Where she…and I'm reading *your* words here," she says, an accusation. "'Damian takes her into his arms. Damian: Never forget that you are mine.' That doesn't happen in that scene."

No, it's not. Baldwin had written:

*"I have to go." I sniff miserably. Why won't he touch me? Why should I stay if he doesn't want me near him?*

*His eyes blaze with fury. "Because that man says you have to?"*

*"He's not just 'that man'. He's my boss." Will Damian ever understand that I'm not choosing Jackson over him? "I'll lose my job."*

*"You don't need a job. I have enough money that you never have to work another day in your life. You just don't want to take it. What is it about that man, that you can't stay away from him?" Damian asks, and the chill in his voice*

*frightens me. His jealousy makes him unpredictable; I'm afraid of what he'll do.*

*"I-I told you," I stammer helplessly, taking a step back. "He's my boss."*

*Damian grabs me by the shoulders. He shakes me violently, his face twisted in furious passion, and I wince in pain. "You. Are. Mine!" he shouts into my face, and I am helpless in his hold. I melt against him and my lips part, willing. Wanting.*

There was absolutely no way I could put that on the screen. Not without turning it into a remake of *Sleeping with The Enemy.*

"I know it isn't," I tell her. "But without being privy to her internal monologue, we're not going to see how she truly feels about him, and why. On screen, he'll just be shaking her and screaming at her."

"Shouting," Lynn corrects me. "I never wrote that he screamed at her."

I don't argue with the semantics of a man shouting into his girlfriend's face as opposed to screaming into it. "I just feel like we need to see why she would want to have sex with him immediately after that exchange."

"And this," she goes on, as if I haven't spoken, and pushes a page across the table to me. "None of this is even in the book."

Jack finally steps in. "Occasionally, scenes to need to be added for clarity, or, as Jessica has said, to strengthen the bond between characters—"

"But it isn't in the book," Lynn says, looking between the two of us as though we were arguing that two plus two equaled one-hundred.

"The aftercare scene is less than a page long. There isn't even any dialogue," I point out. "It's just there so we can see the caring that Ella feels from Damian, without hearing her words in our head."

Lynn frowns. "I'm not sure you're interpreting this text from the correct paradigm. In in the next scene, he takes her out and buys her diamonds."

"And that's very nice of him." My eyes flick to Jack's, and I wish they hadn't. He's not pleased with how the exchange is going, but Lynn's the one with near-total creative control. He wants me to back off. But how? If I give, now, over the very first clash, we might as well let Lynn write, direct, and star in the movie herself.

I clear my throat. "The diamonds are still in play. But I do think we need the added aftercare scene. It's only a minute or two, tops. Damian is an experienced Dom, and aftercare is an important part of that. Without it—"

"Are you suggesting I didn't research my subject matter?" Her eyes narrow to blades aimed directly at me.

I know for a fact that she hasn't, at least, not with any depth, but the way she's glaring at me makes the hairs on the back of my neck stand up. "Not at all. I'm just trying to make sure your vision reaches the screen in exactly the way you hoped."

"I had hoped it would reach the screen in exactly the way I wrote it," she huffs. Her phone chimes, and without so much as an "excuse me", she takes the call, leaving us to sit awkwardly while she puts it on speaker phone.

"Kathy?"

"Just a quick update on Dakota's English paper. Her tutor isn't quite finished with it—"

"What am I paying her for, then?" Lynn snaps. "That needs to be in her teacher's inbox by three if she's going to get full credit."

"Okay. I'll finish it myself," Kathy says, and I can almost see the grim determination in her voice transforming into a pinched facial expression. "I'm on the way to pick you up, right now. I'm at the studio gate. Shouldn't be more than five minutes."

"Perfect." Lynn fixes her gaze on me. "We're not making any progress here, anyway."

I sit up straighter. Did she just talk about me in front of me?

She ends the call, then says to me, "Look, I understand what's happening here. *Beautiful Darkness* is a very successful book. It's only natural that you'd want to put your artistic flare into it, to be a part of it in some way. But it's mine. No one knows this story and these characters better than I do. You must absolutely listen to me on this. I know what my readers want."

I don't bother to explain to her that it won't just be her passionate readers viewing the film. It will be the people whose friends or partners read the book and convinced them to go. It will be the people who heard only negative press, people who read the book and hated it. *Beautiful Darkness* is the most talked about novel of the year, and there will be people waiting to rip the movie—and anyone associated with it—apart.

"I think we need a little space here," Jack says, trying to mediate. "We understand your concerns, Lynn, but Jessica is a very talented screenwriter. I wouldn't have trusted her with this project if I didn't believe in her work, or if I thought she didn't believe in yours. Your concerns are valid. Of course you want the story you love to please the people who love it. But why don't you wait for the completed script? We can go over it then, with Marion. She might be able to offer some fresh perspective."

Marion Cross has been tapped to direct; *Deadline* announced it this morning. I like Marion. She's made some great films. Too many great films to direct this one. She must owe Jack a monumentally huge favor.

A lot of people do.

Lynn makes a noise of reluctant acceptance. "Fine. Let me know when it's finished."

She stands and sweeps from the conference room without saying goodbye to either of us.

"That was fun," I say under my breath, and meet Jack's expression. I expect him to be annoyed. I just don't expect him to be annoyed with *me*.

"What?" I ask defensively.

He grimaces. "I don't know if you've noticed, but we're working with a woman who's a bit of a control freak."

"I thought I handled myself pretty well." Why is he mad at me? I'm not the one who acted spoiled and sullen.

"You did," he agrees, then immediately reverses it by adding, "if she had been anyone but a suddenly-famous first-time author who can't let go of her baby."

"She let go of her baby the second she signed the contract," I remind him. "Actually, she sold her baby."

"I know. But, when you're writing this, keep in mind that what you think about the book isn't what her readers think. They're expecting to see the Damian Bennet they're fantasizing about during tub time."

"Okay, first of all, that's deeply misogynistic. Just because the book has sex in it doesn't mean women are only reading it for the sexy bits." If they are, I pity them; it has to be hard to rub one out to sentences like, *"His hand reaches the edge of my panties. Oh, god, he's going to touch my privates."* There isn't a lot there to get an engine revving.

"Second," I go on, "the Damian Bennet they fantasize about is going to come off as an even bigger psycho if we put what's in the book on the screen. The only thing that redeems him even slightly is how Ella feels about him. And that's going to be gone."

"You don't like the book," Jack says, like it's the first time he's realized it.

"No, I don't." It's also the first time I've admitted it to him aloud.

"Then, why do you want to adapt it?"

"Well, the paycheck is nice. So is the credit." That part should be obvious. Less obvious is my secondary motivation. "This book is bringing something out in women that, frankly, I don't like. And I can't rewrite *Beautiful Darkness* to change their minds. But maybe I can mitigate some of the damage."

He doesn't say anything, and I think he's going to fire me, so I can't stop talking.

"You know there are problems with the way the lifestyle is presented," I say, lowering my voice.

"There are. And I know why you added the scene you did. And I'm going to fight for you, as much as I can," he promises. "But we're not off to a good start here. From now on, you don't speak directly to Baldwin, okay? Send pages to me, she can talk to you through me, and I'll creatively omit the things that might set her off. At least, until we can get Marion onboard with us."

"Fine." My face burns with anger. Jack has to placate the woman who has near-total creative control of this movie, or risk running into costly delays. I understand that. But I don't understand why he can't have my back on this. All he would have to do is turn on his movie star charm, and she'd be putty in his hands.

I push my temper down. "Do you think Marion will be on board?"

He tilts his head. "I think Marion knows that there's an expectation of failure going into this thing. It's not fair, not to Lynn or her readers, but people are dying to hate on this movie."

"Yeah, and she's not dumb," I agree. "She won't want this to bring her down, too."

"You talk like you all signed on for a hostage rescue, not a guaranteed hit movie." He tries to make it sound like a joke. He fails.

I give him a minute to suffer in the awkwardness with me. Then, I ask, "Why did you sign on for this?"

He shrugs. "The money. And Macrocosm knew they could get Baldwin to sign if I was involved. I mean, after all, I'm Damian Bennet."

"If you were Damian Bennet, I'd toss you across the room." I shake my head and slip the stack of discarded pages into my bag.

Jack holds out his hand. "No, give them here, I'll shred them."

"Ah, the supreme secrecy of *Beautiful Darkness*." I give them over reluctantly. The pages are saved to my hard drive, obviously, and I know that it's nothing personal, but after the confrontation with Lynn, I still feel raw. The idea of my rejected pages grinding through a shredder feels like a judgment.

The fact that it's Jack feeding them in is even worse.

\* \* \* \*

"You have to tell me, right now. What is she like?"

Sherri David, my best L.A. friend, sits on my couch, her bare feet pulled up in a pose made possible only by yoga and the grace of a bendable god. She holds out her glass for another splash of white wine, which I pour carefully. Never a full glass at a time, because for some reason, Sherri thinks drinking the whole bottle a little at a time is less of a sin against her diet than going all-in.

Sherri's an actress in a successful network sitcom, complete with laugh track. She's the Latina bombshell with perfectly pushed up tits who drops innocent innuendos for the rest of her single white twenty-something friends to react to. She's thirty-nine and has been playing twenty-five since she was eighteen.

I sit on the couch next to her and drink straight from the bottle. "She's not as bad as some of the blind items out there might suggest."

Sherri raises an eyebrow.

"But she isn't as 'aww shucks' Midwestern friendly like she comes across in interviews," I relent. I don't want to tell her about what happened today. She doesn't like Jack or my weird relationship with him. She doesn't trust him, needlessly, on my behalf. And she really hates my idea of taking the project on.

But she's the only person I can really vent to, so I go on. "She saw some of the pages I wrote, and she went full-on diva."

Sherri braces herself with an arm on the back of the couch as she leans in closer. "Tell me everything."

"You read the book," I begin.

She cuts me off. "No. I started reading the book. Then, I stopped reading the book."

I wave my hand. "You know what's in the book. You've heard me complain about it at length."

She tilts her head in agreement. "Fair enough."

"Well, I tried to add a tiny, tiny scene where Damian does something nurturing for Ella, and she flipped out. Because him buying Ella diamonds is apparently aftercare enough."

Sherri grimaces.

Weirdly, I find myself apologizing for Lynn. "Writing is a sensitive thing, though. She's miffed that I'm messing with her baby."

"She can be miffed." Sherri rolls her glass between her palms. "I understand that. Did she not like that you were adding to her words, or—"

"Nope." I shake my head firmly. "I used all of her dialogue. I just changed the tone."

"Hmmm." Sherri's mouth screws to the side. "What's your boss think?"

She won't mention Jack by name.

"He's not as totally on my side as I would like him to be," I admit.

Sherri doesn't say anything. She just gives me a grim, sympathetic smile.

My phone buzzes on the coffee table. The screen lights up. It's Kathy the assistant.

"Holy shit." I reach for the phone and almost fumble it by mistake. "I can't believe she's calling me at home."

Sherri starts to respond, but I hold up one finger as I answer the call. "Hello?"

"Hello, this is Kathy Muller, Lynn Baldwin's assistant," she states stiffly, followed by, "I have Ms. Baldwin for you."

Before I can ask what it's about or even say I can take the call, Lynn is on the line. "Jessica? It's Lynn Baldwin."

*Yes, I know that.* "Hi, Lynn. What can I do for you?"

"Actually, it's what I can do for you," she says and sighs. "I am so sorry for the way I acted this afternoon. That was really not okay."

"It's fine." I don't know why I say that. It's not fine.

"I think I'm just intimidated," she goes on. "You're a professional writer, and here I am, just a soccer mom from Oklahoma. I'm worried about looking foolish, because here is this person who does this for a living, when I just do it as a fun hobby."

My hackles raise at that. Not that she finds me intimidating or holds my experience in high esteem, but because all that experience means dick when you compare our paychecks. I love writing, but I would be able to love it more if that love wasn't motivated by fear of homelessness. Lynn would never have to write another word again if the mood didn't strike her.

"Anyway, I'm sorry, I acted awfully today. Can I make it up to you?" she asks.

I don't know what she has in mind, but I'm pretty sure she won't make it up to me by not throwing any more hissy fits. That said, it's nice to know she's able to apologize when she's in the wrong. "What do you have in mind?"

"Well, first of all, I'm going to follow Jack's advice and see what Marion thinks about your new scene." She says this as though she's doing me a generous favor. "And I wanted to know if you'd like to go to a party tomorrow night."

"A party?" The last thing I can imagine myself doing is hanging out at some boring wine and cheese night.

"It's at Jason McEwan's house," she tells me with a girlish giggle. "We're trying to get him to sign on as Damian."

Jason McEwan is a fan favorite for the role, according to the blogs. Instagram is covered with photos of him posing shirtless in magazine shoots, photoshopped with quotes from the books. Jason is as close to Jack-ten-years-ago as Lynn is going to get.

"Well, he must be pretty interested, if he's inviting you over for a house party," I say, to bolster her confidence. If the problem is that she's feeling overwhelmed by the Hollywood-ness of the whole process, it could be cleared up by making her feel as if she belongs. She does. It's her movie, after all.

"Jack got me the invitation. I don't flatter myself that I'm hip enough to hang out with the kids these days." She laughs. "My daughter is so jealous."

"I'll be she is." McEwan is the hot teen werewolf all the girls love. Once he gets away from teen TV drama, the sky is the limit. "I hope you don't think I have any pull with him, though. If that's why you're asking me to come along."

"No, no, not at all," she says quickly. "No, you'd be going as my guest. It sounds like a lot of fun. Lots of celebrities."

I see enough celebrities these days that it's not that exciting a prospect. Still, she sounds so genuine, and she's trying to extend an olive branch. It's going to be a pretty rough few months if I don't try to get along just because we had one minor spat. "Okay, sure. Just have your assistant text me the details."

"Oh, I absolutely will. Well, I won't take you away from my script any longer." She laughs, and I can't tell if she really thinks I'm chained to my desk working on a Friday night. After a bit of pause, she says, softer, "Thank you. For being so understanding."

"It's no problem," I reassure her. When the call ends, I slide my phone onto the table like I'm worried it'll explode.

"What was that about?" Sherri asks, her eyes wide.

"It was Lynn Baldwin. Inviting me to a party at Jason McEwan's house." The sentence is so ridiculous, I snicker.

"What?" Sherri sits back quickly.

"She said Jack got her an invitation."

"Oh, of course he did." Sherri rolls her eyes.

That gives me pause. "What do you mean by that?"

"I mean she probably asked him to get her the invitation," she says, pushing her dark chestnut hair over her shoulder.

"Nah." I begin reluctantly. Then, I think about it, and it does kind of make sense. Why would Jack get her into a random party out of the blue? He doesn't do things like that. And he hates parties.

Sherri puts her empty glass on the coffee table. "Is this really what you want?" she asks, her tone sympathetic.

"The job? Yes. The middle school bullshit?" I shrug. "If I have to go through the latter to keep the former, I will."

For the thousandth time, she says, defeated, "You're so much better than this."

That's what I've been telling myself. And maybe that's the problem.

"I'm really not." Before she can protest, I barrel on. "Yeah, I've written some movies. Over half of everything I've written has never sold. About three quarters of what has sold has never made it to the screen. I might not like *Beautiful Darkness*, but Lynn Baldwin obviously knows what it takes to be a success."

"Success and talent aren't even in the same neighborhood."

I know she's trying to cheer me up. It doesn't work.

Jenny Trout

November 14, 2007

It took me seventy-two hours to get up the courage to email Jack Martin. Now, I'm sitting in the living room of a hillside mansion that cost more than I could make in twenty lifetimes, watching him uncork a bottle of wine at his wet bar.

"I still can't believe your name is Jessica," he says, shaking his head. "I had you built up to be…"

"To be what?" I prompt him, shifting nervously on the sofa. It's one of those perfectly structured pieces of furniture that's comfortable, yet easy to sit on without sinking too far in.

"I don't know. Victoria? Genevieve?" He chuckles to himself as he pours. "Something regal. Jessica is kind of plain."

"Your name is Jack," I remind him dryly.

He shrugs and smiles and comes toward me with the two glasses. "Yeah, okay. Point taken."

Handing me a glass, he sits beside me on the couch and gestures to the stack of printed pages sitting on the coffee table. My pages. My words, in Jack Martin's house.

"So, this is good," he says, taking a drink of his wine before he places it carefully on the glass-topped table. "The screenplay. Not the—"

"I knew what you meant," I interject. My knees are weak. Because it's nerve wracking to have someone else read your writing, not because he's Jack.

Okay, it's kind of because he's Jack.

It seems like every five seconds, I'm struck again that I'm sitting in Jack Martin's living room, drinking wine and talking about my script with Jack Martin. Movie star, Jack Martin. I take a big swallow of wine before I try to speak without sounding like a total nervous wreck. "I'm relieved."

"I have some feedback, if you don't mind." He flips through pages, and it takes everything in me to not shout enthusiastically that of course I don't mind.

"Yeah, sure," I say, trying to sound casual.

"I think your second act drags." The bluntness with which he says it eases a big fear that I had in coming here. I was afraid this was all a come on, that since I'm a sex worker, I'm automatically easy, that all it will take is a little flattery, and my legs will magically snap open.

Not that I wouldn't have sex with Jack Martin. Even just for the story. And I've got a theory that good-looking men are terrible in bed because they think they don't have to try. He would be the perfect addition to my data.

But he's actually invested in discussing my script, and it only takes a few minutes before I'm leaning in eagerly, my eyes flicking over the pages he's holding as he gives me examples.

"This entire section here," he says, drawing his finger over a page before flipping to the next and doing the same. "You could easily reduce this. You have a habit of making your characters repeat each other?"

"Repeat each other?"

"Exactly like that," he says, pointing at me. "You've also got a point in here… Where was it…"

As he searches for it, I watch his brow crumple in concentration. "Okay, the exposition here is clunky. Whenever you have a character saying, 'as you know,' at the beginning of a sentence, that's a dead giveaway that you're about to dump a lot of information into our laps. There are smoother ways to work this in." He looks up at me. "Did you see *The Queen*?"

Of course I had. It had been nominated for too many major awards to ignore it. "Yeah."

"So, you know that very first scene, where Helen Mirren says she envies the painter because he can vote, and it would be nice to be able to experience that just once? Then, the painter comes in and says something like, 'one forgets that as sovereign, her Majesty is not entitled to vote,' or something like that?" He waits for me to nod before he continues. "The part where she says it would be nice to check the box, to be partisan, that was enough. It didn't need the follow up to explain to the viewer that she can't vote. They already said it."

"So, basically, don't beat people over the head with it?" I gnaw my lip, then remember that I'm wearing lipstick and have probably smeared it all over my teeth.

"Don't beat people over the head with it, and definitely don't have a character tell another character something that second character already knows. It takes you out of the moment. It feels like..." He pauses as if struggling for the words.

But I know what he's going to say, because I see it in the pages he holds in front of him. "Like the characters are aware of the audience."

He snaps his fingers. "Exactly."

"Is this something all actors can do?" I know I'm taking the conversation off track, but I can't help but wonder if he's interested in screenwriting, himself. "Dissect something like this, I mean?"

"Maybe," he says, his tone flat.

It doesn't leave me much to respond to.

"People don't tend to take you seriously about this stuff when you're just there to do stunts and look pretty." The bitterness in his tone is palpable.

"So, are you looking to branch out? Write something of your own?" It's a personal question, and I feel a little strange asking it. But he'd opened up to me like I was Oprah in the strip club lounge all those years ago. Maybe I'm overstepping, but he seems like the kind of person who needs prodding before they'll talk, and it feels like he wants—or needs—to talk about this.

It takes him so long to respond that I'm afraid I've really, really offended him. When he does speak, it sounds carefully rehearsed. "I'm happy being an actor. It's an honor to bring a writer's words to life, to bring a director's vision to life."

I don't know what compels me to keep pushing, but I wish it would stop. My face is hot with embarrassment, but I can't control my mouth. "Is that your real answer, or the one you give to interviewers?"

He sighs. "You caught me."

Another long silence. I'm sure he'll kick me out of his house at any moment. Then, he says, "I just want someone to see that I can do more than just say cheesy lines and walk away from explosions."

"Have you written anything of your own?" I ask gently.

He shakes his head. "Not much of a writer myself. But I could direct a movie. I know I could. It's been driving me insane, trying to work with these guys who think carefully about positioning actresses so their tits and ass can be seen at the same time, but won't listen when we complain that the dialogue is stilted."

"The tits and ass kind of sell the movies, though," I remind him. "Not to downplay your role in *Last Man Standing,* but Danica Wolfe's cleavage in the previews got a lot of butts in seats."

He laughs grimly. "Yeah. And I get scripts like that all the time. 'In this one, you're a CIA assassin who teams up with a sexy KGB agent to stop a global terrorist.' 'In this one, you're a hit man who learns that his sexy target is marked for extermination because she knows too much about the government's plan to release Ebola into the New York City water source.'"

My mouth falls open. "That can't be a real movie."

"I'm exaggerating," he admits. "But only by a little. I understand why people like action movies. Everyone wants to be a hero, right? But I can do more, and I feel like everyone only sees me as the meathead explosion guy."

"Meathead Explosion would be a great band name."

"Or a very gross cause of death." He drops my screenplay on the table to rub both hands down his face. "I'm sorry. I didn't bring you here to be my career counselor."

"It's okay. People tell me I'm a good listener." Too good, sometimes. "You wouldn't believe what some guys have unloaded on me."

He turns his face toward me and gives me a small, crooked smile. "If the worst thing about you is that you're too empathetic, you're doing pretty good."

"Plus, you know I'm not going to blab my mouth." I don't know why I say it. Maybe because he mentioned it in the VIP room that first night we met. Maybe because he thanked me for it a few days ago. But there's something that seems so vulnerable about him.

If I were a different person, he might make a great character in a screenplay.

He gives me a small, grateful smile and picks up my pages, again. "So, where were we on this?"

"Why don't you?" I ask suddenly.

"Why don't I what?"

"Now, you're the one doing the repeating." I smile and look down at my hands in my lap. "You want to direct something? Why not ask?"

His frown fully dismisses the idea. "That's not how it works."

"Why shouldn't it be?" I can't imagine that a guy who pulls in the kind of money he does at the box office isn't being offered carte blanche at his studio. "You're a big deal, Jack. You're one of the most powerful guys in Hollywood, right now. If you haven't already approached a studio about the possibility, they should have already come to you."

"I'm worth more to them on the poster than behind the camera," he says gloomily. "And believe me, that doesn't feel powerful. It feels subservient."

"You'll never know if you don't ask." It's the last I'll say on the subject. I don't want to sound pushy, and I realize with shock that it's not because I don't want to mess up my chances at getting my script passed on to someone else important. It's because I don't want to ruin Jack's trust in me. Because he does seem to trust me, if he's willing to spill his guts like this.

He studies me for a moment, his expression inscrutable. "You're very good at this. Have you ever considered giving up dancing to become a therapist? Or a motivational speaker."

"Well, I did give up dancing," I admit. What the hell? He told me a bunch of personal stuff, I can be honest about my job. "I'm a professional dominatrix, now."

His eyebrows lift. "Oh."

"But, no, I wouldn't give it up to become a therapist. I know what I want to do, and I'm not going to settle for anything less."

"What if you don't make it?" he asks, and I know he's not asking about me.

"I'd rather work my whole life at something I love and never get anywhere than give up now and wonder 'what if'."

He considers for a moment, then turns back to the script in front of him. "Can I give you a spoiler for the future?"

"Sure."

He picks up the pages and flicks the first one with his fingers. "You're not going to fail."

## Chapter Four

Jason McEwan lives in a house that's way too large for one man, and way too small for the party happening in it. I wait in the valet line for what seems like hours; they're having a hard time finding places to park.

When I finally reach the gate, I give the security guy my name, and he scans the list doubtfully. He finds me, but criticizes me with his gaze; he doesn't think I'm worthy to be in this crowd.

Truth be told, I'm really not worthy. The world beyond this sentry is the realm of young Hollywood; the ultra-modern white mansion is a fortress of cool, and the people crowded under the cantilevered roof are at the threshold of a future they're poised to dominate.

The trap music playing inside spills out the front door as I enter. Six feet into the house, the star of the latest YA inspiration porn adaptation spills her ass across the marble foyer and laughs hysterically, loud enough to drown out the music. I try not to make eye contact with a few people who clearly think I'm crashing, and hold my head high as I scan the crowd for any sign of Jack or Lynn. It's hard to tell if I'm overdressed or underdressed based on what I see as I wander deeper into the house. There are women dressed for the nightclub and guys dressed for the tennis court. Suit jackets with no ties, faded t-shirts and Converse. I cross paths with a woman in a green sequined string bikini and a cheap costume store war bonnet as she runs inside from the pool, where I assume some gratuitous nudity is taking place. I've tried to be hip, without looking like mutton-dressed-as-lamb, as my grandmother used to say. A blousy silk halter dress belted with tasseled cord and paired with delicate lace-up sandals just doesn't feel right here, though.

I realize, too late, that it's the person wearing it that makes it stuffy. I'm twenty years older than some of these people.

I step out onto the pool deck and spot Jack standing near the bar. He's perfectly at ease in his dark blue suit, like he just came back from a red carpet premiere; it's more likely that he's come straight from work. The light is strange out here, the full moon competing with the glow from the underwater fixtures and the long strip of flaming fireplace that divides the swimming pool down its length. One minute, Jack looks like something out of an on-screen love scene; the next, like the cold, steely guy he pretends to be.

He leans in toward the gorgeous blond he's talking to. When she turns her head, I recognize her. Madison Avery, a twenty-something actress from a cable drama. I'm not surprised to see her here, but I am surprised at the look on Jack's face as he excuses himself from the conversation.

Lynn appears at my side as silently as the angel of death. "He's smitten with her."

"I can understand that." Fresh-faced, perfect nose, almost too many teeth, her slender body poured into the tight white dress she wears… I would hit on Madison Avery, if I had less shame and a hard-on for much younger women.

But I don't want to discuss it, so I change the subject. "Did you just get here?"

Lynn shakes her head and sips something bright orange from her glass. "I've been here for a little while, now, but I'm still looking for our host."

As she scans the crowded pool deck, Jack approaches us. "Lynn, Jessica. I suppose you're wondering why I gathered you all here tonight."

"Is that a joke?" I feign suspicion. "What's in that glass?"

"Trouble." He takes another sip.

"So," Lynn begins, wheedling. "I don't suppose you could help me find our host?"

Jack's brow creases. "I'm sure he's around here somewhere. He's very social and good at circulating, you're bound to run into him."

"I meant—" Lynn lowers her voice and leans toward him, too conspicuous, "—I wanted to talk to him about the movie."

"The movie?"

"Yes, the movie. I want to talk to him about being *in* the movie," she says, her lips pursing as though she's pulled one over on us, and we're supposed to think she's very clever.

Jack doesn't like clever. "That's not really your department. If you want the casting director to consider him, fine, but you can't just offer him the part. I thought I made that clear when we talked earlier."

Lynn's expression freezes. "I have creative control."

"You have *some* creative control." He leans on the operative word. "And we haven't even begun casting, yet."

"We've been floating names," she asserts. "Is there really any harm in letting Jason know that his is one of them?"

"Isn't there?" Jack fires back neutrally, but I know neutral won't last, and soon, they'll be shouting at each other in the middle of the party. "There are things we have to consider. Like whether or not he's within the budget."

"It's not a terrible idea," I interject, before they can both destroy themselves. "I mean, obviously, don't make any promises. But it couldn't hurt to at least gauge his reaction to the project."

"Then, it's settled," Lynn says, and gestures to the half-empty glass in her hand. "I'm going to go get this freshened up, and we can find him together."

When she's out of earshot, Jack turns to me. "Gauge his reaction to the project?"

I shrug. "It's clearly why she wanted to be here tonight. Nobody our age wants to be here tonight." Except for maybe Jack, whose eyes keep straying to the blond goddess near the bar. Madison is charming another man, now, and Jack seems intent on monitoring the situation.

71

I ask him, "Did you offer Lynn the invite, or did she ask you for one?"

"She asked," he admits guiltily. "She said she overheard someone talking about it at Macrocosm."

"And you figured she just wanted to go to a random stranger's party?"

"That random stranger is a celebrity," Jack reminds me.

"Right. But a celebrity that her online fan club has already adopted as the unofficial face of Damian Bennett." Because I can't resist, I add, "No matter which celebrity *she* might have been thinking of when she wrote all those torrid love scenes."

A flush creeps above his open collar, and he hides his discomfort with a swallow of the dark amber liquid in his glass. "Let's say she does get a few moments with him tonight, and it doesn't go well."

"Like, she offers him the role outright? He's a professional, Jack. He knows she doesn't have that kind of power. Any damage she does in that arena can be quickly undone."

I assume.

"No, I mean, what if she meets him, and he's not as fawning and gracious as she'll expect him to be?" Jack angles himself away from the bar and lowers his voice. "I don't think it's escaped your notice that this has gone to her head a little. The studio has coddled her, but Jason McEwan is under no obligation to do so."

"If he wants the part, he is."

"If he wants the part," Jack repeats. "I think Lynn is assuming that he will. If we set her up for disappointment without knowing how she'll react—"

"Hey!" I say brightly past his shoulder to alert him to Lynn's return.

She beams at us. "So, shall we go and find him, then?"

Jack gives a sideways nod to the house, and we follow him back inside, through the big double doors. Green bikini girl runs past us, again, shouting someone's name.

"This is wild," Lynn says, in what would have been a conspiratorial whisper, if it could be heard over the blasting music. "I always suspected Hollywood parties were like this."

"They're not. I mean, not always." This kind of debauchery is exactly the type of shit I like to avoid.

"But the important ones are," she decides firmly.

Jack leads us into a den, where Jason and other partygoers are piled onto a huge L-shaped couch. Despite the volume of the music over the speakers, the television holds them transfixed with a showing of *Pacific Rim*, sans sound. The huge bong they're passing around explains some of the tableau.

"Jack! Hey, man, you wanna hit this?" Blue smoke curls from Jason's mouth as he speaks. He turns his hand upside down when he points to the bong.

Jack holds up a hand. "Currently abstaining. Do you have a second?"

"For you? Yeah." Jason passes the pipe off and stands. "Let's go upstairs."

As Jason leads the way, Jack introduces us.

"This is Jessica Yates. She's a screenwriter," he explains.

"Yeah, *Still Waters,* right?" Jason shakes his head. "Man, that was a good movie. I had to watch it twice. Blew my mind."

"Thanks, I'm glad you liked it," I say.

In a heartbeat, Lynn interjects, "Jack directed that, you know."

"Yeah, I did know." Jason holds up his fist to bump against Jack's. "We're bros, aren't we, Jack?"

"I don't have bros," Jack says dryly. "This is Lynn Baldwin. She is also a writer."

"A screenwriter?" Jason asks, looking to all of us for confirmation.

"A novelist," Lynn says. There's a bit of an edge in her voice.

The weed Jason smoked appears to have dulled that edge, because he says cheerfully, "Right on. Anything I would have read?"

I swear I feel a draft blowing off Lynn's expression.

"Lynn wrote *Beautiful Darkness.* You've heard of it," Jack says smoothly.

"Right, right. The whip me, spank me book." Jason laughs. "That's cool, that's cool. Thanks for stopping by my party. Maybe you can put in a good word for me with some of the girls here. Say it was inspired by me."

"Funny you should mention that," Lynn says, and Jack silences her with a look.

I just can't believe Jason doesn't search his name on Instagram. He would know *all* about *Beautiful Darkness* if he did.

Jason takes us to a room that looks more like an art gallery than a part of someone's house. Three huge canvases form one abstract piece marbled in yellow, green, and blue. It's even lit with gallery-style track lights. The floor in the room is polished concrete, the walls stark white. The glass wall gives us a view of the pool below. For some reason, my eyes seek out Madison Avery. When I don't see her, I check to make sure Jack doesn't see her, either. But he's not even facing the windows.

"Have a seat, guys," Jason says, motioning to the padded benches in the middle of the room. They're arranged around a glossy jet-black coffee table, but I doubt anyone uses the room to kick back and put their feet up. "What do you want to talk about?"

"Lynn here…" Jack begins, and pauses. "Actually, Lynn, why don't you tell him?"

She wastes no time. "First, let me just say thank you for having me in your beautiful home."

Jason nods. "No problem."

"I'm not sure if you're aware, but my book—*Beautiful Darkness,*" she emphasizes, "—is currently the bestselling novel in the entire world."

"Sex sells. Right, Jack?' Jason holds his fist out, again, and Jack reluctantly bumps knuckles with him over the table.

"It is so much more than a sex book." Lynn looks to Jack and me for backup, but I have no idea what she wants me to say. When it's apparent that no help is coming, Lynn goes on. "The book has attracted a lot of fans, and they're all in love with the main character, Damian Bennet."

"Uh huh," Jason says slowly.

"They meet online to talk about the book, to write fan fiction. They make fan casts." She's waiting for any recognition of fandom phenomenon from him, but it's just not there.

"A lot of readers have you in mind when they're reading the book," Jack says bluntly.

Jason's spine straightens, and he blinks as he processes what that means. "Wow. Well, that's flattering."

"It absolutely is," Lynn says, hurrying to take up the reins. "Damian Bennett is every woman's fantasy."

I can't help the glance that flicks to Jack. He's already giving me the eyebrow warning.

"I guess that's not the worst thing someone could think of me," Jason says with a laugh. It takes him another second to get why we're actually there. "Hey, um, aren't you guys doing a movie or something?"

"Macrocosm acquired the rights. We're in development, right now." Jack says this noncommittally.

"Jessica is writing a phenomenal script," Lynn says, looping an arm around my shoulders. I resist on impulse, but go limp and accept it when I realize she's not letting go.

"*You're* writing it?" Jason makes a face. "Why?"

The silence is enough to induce tinnitus.

Lynn's arm slithers off of me, and Jason tries to smooth things over. "What I meant was, I've seen a couple movies that you've written. Why are you adapting something?"

"Change of pace." I just want to get this conversation speeding in the opposite direction from where it was headed. "And so many people love it. When Jack offered me the project, I jumped at the chance to do right by the fans."

"Of course, that was all with my approval." Lynn sniffs.

"We've given Lynn a lot of creative control in the process," Jack says. It's a warning. A flashing neon sign urging Jason to run.

"Yes, I have a lot of input over things like the script." She inclines her head toward me. "And the casting."

This is exactly what Jack didn't want her to do. He's going to be furious. I see the vein behind his jaw tick. I see that vein a lot, usually when he's trying to hold a scream in.

My hand comes up to touch my own throat before I can stop myself.

Jason puts his hands on his knees and pushes back a little. "Okay. Awkward."

He drags the sound out in the most painfully second-hand embarrassing way. I want to shrivel up into the bench.

"I don't see how it's awkward," Lynn says. "I would think it was a compliment."

Jason shakes his head. "You might think it's a compliment, but believe me, it's awkward knowing that millions of women are fantasizing about me beating them up."

"No one is getting beaten up," Lynn snaps.

"It's BDSM. It's a sexual fetish. Totally consensual," Jack says in an effort to intervene.

Jason isn't budging. "It sounds sick. And I'm sorry, I'm not going to be the poster boy for whips and chains. Is that why you came tonight, Jack? Because you wanted to test the waters? You know me better than that, bro."

My tongue feels thick in my mouth, my stomach hollow. Sick? I know that's what some people think of BDSM, but hearing it come from someone whose house is a full-on Roman orgy makes it sting a little more.

"We didn't come to test the waters," Jack asserts, but there's no use. It's already happened. Jack can't stuff Lynn's remark about casting back into the bottle.

Jason scoffs. "Bullshit, Jack. Come on. Everyone knows this thing is a joke. It's all just shit for soccer moms to rub off to. There's no staying power. It's already a punchline. I'd have to owe you a pretty fucking big favor to sign on to that."

The look on Lynn's face breaks my heart. I might not think *Beautiful Darkness* is the important literary masterpiece that she thinks it is, but there's no reason for Jason to be so openly cruel. I flinch inwardly, imagining how I would feel if someone said those things to me. How Lynn isn't crying, right now, is beyond me.

And I'm pissed at Jack. Sure, he'd warned her to watch her step, and she'd basically offered Jason the role, right then, but Jack knew who she was. He knew she wasn't as polished and savvy as she pretended to be. Only eighteen months ago, she'd been cutting the crusts off of PB&Js and driving her kids to after-school activities. This was a whole different world, and he expected her to navigate it like Magellan.

I'm the only one in the situation who doesn't have anything to lose, so I speak up. "It's not a favor. The movie is a guaranteed blockbuster. The promotion is going to put the faces of whoever wind up as Damian and Ella on thousands of billboards, posters, magazine ads... It's going to be a world-wide phenomenon."

"It's going to be an embarrassment." Jason stands. "Look, I suppose I should say that I appreciate you thinking of me. Enjoy the party."

Then, he leaves us there in his weird miniature art gallery to find our own way out.

Nobody speaks until he's long gone. Then, just as Lynn sighs in preparation, Jack says, "That was specifically what I asked you not to do."

"I didn't do anything," she says, pressing a hand to her chest in outrage. "We were having a nice chat, then he suddenly—"

"Then, you suddenly offered him the role." Before she can talk, again, he adds, "Don't say you didn't offer anything, just because the words 'would you like to play Damian Bennett?' didn't come out of your mouth. I advised you not to do this, and you deliberately ignored that advice."

"Oh, he knew exactly why you wanted to get him alone and talk to me," she accuses Jack. "This is how deals are done all the time here."

"Not the way I do them!" He pushes up from the bench and stalks in a slow circle.

"Okay, okay," I say, standing myself. I have to play peacemaker or Jack is going to make everything so much worse. "Lynn, you're right. It probably was totally obvious to Jason that you we were angling for him. But you did put him on the spot."

"He could have reacted more graciously!" she protests.

"He didn't have the chance!" Jack rakes a hand through his hair. "What he said? He might have said that to me if we offered him the role. But he would have said it in private, instead of right here in front of you while we all die of second-hand embarrassment."

She looks as though she's been pushed down a flight of stairs and is only realizing it on the way down. "How dare you?"

"How dare I? I brought you here, to meet one of my acquaintances, because you wanted to go to some big Hollywood party. I have news for you, Lynn, but this is not a theme park. This is not a vacation for us. We're trying to do our jobs while you have your Cinderella moment—"

Lynn starts sniping back at him, and soon, there is an embarrassing echo in the nearly empty room as their voices rise.

"Enough! That is enough!" I shout, channeling my mother in the midst of a sibling-on-sibling cage match. "The two of you need to separate. Call each other in a couple of days, when you've had time to realize how stupid you both sound, right now, and apologize. We're in this together. The movie won't get made otherwise. And, if you think this was humiliating, just wait until it's *Variety* writing about how it all fell through."

I expect Lynn to fire back with something about how the movie won't get made without her approval or some other ego-fueled nonsense. Instead, she carefully moves a few strands of hair off her red face and says, "I'm going to get another drink."

Jack goes to the window and looks out, but I know he's not seeing the people on the pool deck below. He's seeing money and opportunity and credibility siphoning away. And I know how important those all are, how tied in together they are.

"I should have fucking known better," he says, his expression grim as he stares out at nothing. "I should have trusted my gut."

"I did kind of help you ignore that gut." In hindsight, it was stupid and obvious. Maybe I wanted her to get smacked down a little.

God, was I *that* person? If I set her up for failure because, why, she didn't like my pages? What would that accomplish, other than making everything more difficult for all of us?

"If you're accepting responsibility for this, I'll let you," he says with a grim laugh. "I have to go smooth things over with Jason. Can you take Lynn detail?"

"Yup." I owe that much to all of us.

"I'll probably take off right after I talk to him. I've got an early morning," Jack says. "If I don't see you—"

"I'll assume you said goodbye." I take a few steps back on my way to the door. "I'll email you tomorrow."

"Right."

I turn and leave him there to seek out Lynn.

Just as she indicated I would, I find her near the bar, posing for a selfie with a tan young woman in a white bikini. As I watch their interaction, I take note of their body language. The woman waves her hands in the air in front of her, presses one to her chest. Her smile is wide, and she bounces on the balls of her feet as she talks. All the while, Lynn nods and smiles graciously, hands folded reverently around her drink like Moses' hands on his staff. This, I realize, is what readers see when they look at her; someone who is like them, who craves the same engagement with the world of *Beautiful Darkness* as they do. She didn't just write the book; through her confidence, she gives them the freedom to enjoy it.

I wait until the exchange is over and Lynn moves away before trying to catch her eye. The moment I do, her expression sours. I make my way to her, mentally rehearsing what I want to say.

"Do you have a minute?" I ask her, and indicate some empty armchairs near a less-occupied spot on the deck.

"Of course," she answers, all business.

I lead the way, willing myself not to look behind to make sure she's following. When we reach the chairs, I let her sit first.

"I suppose Jack sent you out here to smooth things over with me?" she says, looking me unflinchingly in the eye.

"Yes. I'm sorry he acted that way," I tell her.

"You know, it isn't so much that Jason was my first choice. It's that he was rude." She shakes her head. "That's what happens with Millennials. They're so used to getting participation ribbons and trophies for losing, they think everything is owed to them. They're ungrateful."

"Uh-huh," I agree superficially, remembering her remark just days ago about her daughter's tutor finishing her homework for her. But once the word "Millennials" is uttered by anyone over thirty-five, there's no point in trying to reason with them. "But I wasn't talking about Jason. I was talking about Jack."

"Oh, him." She blows out a long breath and rolls her eyes. "He's very temperamental. It's one of the reasons he inspired Damian Bennett. But he's certainly not as alpha. If he were, he would have stuck up for me in there."

Jack? Not alpha? I almost laugh aloud. If he wasn't as "alpha" as he is, I wouldn't get off so hard on dominating him. Where would the challenge be?

"Well, you're right, he isn't Damian." Thank god. "But it wasn't his fault things went badly in there."

"I suppose it was mine?" Lynn asks with an arched brow that reminds me that my job is on the line.

*Yes.* "No. It's Jason McEwan's. He decided to be a jerk. But, yeah, your actions gave him the opportunity."

"You can't hold that against me," she all but orders. "Jack knows this is all new to me."

*But he warned you. He gave you instructions.* That's not what she's going to want to hear. "Well, tonight, he got a reminder."

"Maybe you could remind him, too," she suggests. "He'll listen to you."

"I'm just a screenwriter. I have no power here." Hopefully, hearing that will please her, somehow.

"But you're friends, aren't you? He said he was your mentor."

"He is. In a way." My gut roils. I hate for anyone to notice anything particularly close or friendly between Jack and me. "The first film he directed was the first screenplay I sold. He was responsible for me getting to where I am. So, I guess he's more like a benefactor than a mentor."

"Well, he respects you," Lynn grumbles. "He doesn't respect me."

"I wouldn't say that." Not to her face. "But there are a lot of people who want to get this movie made and get it made right. And sometimes, it seems like you're working against us."

"I'm sure it does. But it seems like you're all working against me, too. I know how I want this to look on the screen. And none of you are listening to me."

"I'm sorry you feel that way." It's a non-apology, on purpose. Because the fact of the matter is, we can't listen to her every idea or expectation. Somehow, getting that through to her has become the biggest part of the development process.

I reach into my pocket and pull out my phone. I don't care what time it is. It could be nine, and I would still make an excuse to leave. Luckily, it's quarter to midnight. "I have to go. I write best at night."

"Well, by all means, go. Hop off and add six or seven more scenes to my story," she snaps.

I stand and wait to turn away from her before rolling my eyes. "Jack will have a first draft for you soon, Lynn."

I consider seeking out Jack to say goodbye and to see if he's managed to apologize to Jason. Even though it's clear that Jason McEwan will not be our Damian Bennett, professional relationships have to be maintained. But I change my mind and head for the door. Jack said he was leaving, anyway.

On my way out, I spot him. He's leaning against the deck rail beside Madison Avery. They're talking and looking out at the sparkling lights of the valley below us.

January 16, 2008

## JACK MARTIN ATTACHED TO DIRECT DEBUT WRITER JESSICA YATES'S 'STILL WATERS' FOR MACROCOSM

Macrocosm Studios reports that Jack Martin (*Dangerous Identity*) will direct his first feature film, *Still Waters*, for Macrocosm. The debut screenplay by Jessica Yates follows the residents of Still Waters, GA as they grapple with a string of mysterious drownings. This move is a marked departure for the actor, whose latest feature, *Last Man Standing,* grossed $156m in its opening weekend. Yates is represented by Robert Stewart of IWM.

Jenny Trout

## Chapter Five

It only takes me three more weeks to finish the first draft of *Beautiful Darkness.* I tried not to veer from the roadmap of the book unless it was absolutely necessary, not for my conscience, but for the adaptation of the story. It's still unsettling to me that some of the alarming content might make it to the screen, but I'm banking on Marion Cross to be my Hail Mary.

Sherri has big news for me, so we made a last-minute date to meet for lunch. It helps distract me from worrying about Jack reading the script. He's taking his damn time.

"So, what's the big news?" I ask, after Sherri arrives and we do our greeting hug. Before she can answer, the waitress appears at our table to drop off sparkling water and tell us the specials. It seems to take forever, because I know the look on Sherri's face. Something big, really, super big, is happening.

Finally, the waitress leaves, and Sherri is barely able to contain herself. "*Northwest* is going to Sundance."

"What?" My voice is so loud it disrupts the diners seated near us. "Oh my god, that's fantastic!"

During her break from filming the show, Sherri took a chance and starred in an independent movie about a woman battling heroin addiction. It's gritty and topical; the character is a young woman with a chronic illness who turns to heroin when she loses her health insurance. There's been a lot of buzz about the movie and about Sherri's performance, but it had never seemed destined for wide distribution. At a major festival? It's bound to get picked up.

"Yeah, he actually wasn't going to enter it, because he didn't think we had a chance in hell." Sherri bounces in her chair. "But it's going!"

"Are *you* going?" I ask, a little skeptical. Sherri once said she moved from New York to L.A. so she would never have to see a snowflake, again.

"Of course I am!" She rolls her eyes. "Yes, I know it's in January, and yes, buying winter coats is going to be an expense I really don't need, but I'll be fine. It's the alcohol I'm worried about. Isn't Utah a dry state?"

"I doubt a film festival would be." Leave it to Sherri to worry about the really important stuff. "But what about the show? Are they going to let you take that kind of time?"

She waves a hand. "They'll figure something out. It's not like we didn't work around Alan going to rehab."

"True." I move out of cautious, practical mode and into excited-for-my-friend mode. "This is amazing!"

"I know! I don't want to sound ungrateful for the job I have, but this could mean so much for me. The show isn't going to last forever, and I don't want to end up running away from it for the rest of my career. If I had a parallel career I could transition to—"

"Like Jennifer Aniston," I offer.

"Exactly like Jennifer Aniston." She drums her fingers on the tabletop. "You don't think I'm getting my hopes up too much, do you?"

The waitress appears, again, and while we place our order, I consider Sherri's question. The problem is, I'm not sure Sherri has a setting below "getting my hopes up too much". When the waitress leaves us, I settle on, "You know, get your hopes up as much as you want to. If you try to manage your expectations, it's not going to work, anyway. And you deserve to be excited about this."

"I just don't want to sound too full of myself," she says doubtfully.

I sympathize with that on a deep, deep level. Everyone has worked with someone who thought way too much of their talents or thought they deserved more than anyone else. Nobody wanted to actually *be* that person. "You don't. You're celebrating. You're excited. And you're thinking critically about your future. If you sat down here and started writing your acceptance speech thanking the Academy, then maybe I'd feel a little different."

"And you'll tell me if I my head gets too big?" she asks earnestly.

I laugh. "Oh, I promise you I will tell you if your head gets too big."

She gives herself another little happy dance moment, then gets serious. "Okay, enough about my news. How does La Diva like your tribute to her opus maximus?"

"Magnum opus," I correct her. "And I have no idea. I've got a meeting tomorrow morning with Jack and Marion Cross. I guess I find out, then."

"Rewrites are going to be a nightmare," Sherri says.

"You think I don't know?" I shake my head, not even wanting to imagine the mountain of notes I'll probably have waiting for me tomorrow. "It'll be fine, though. At this point, I just want to get through it and on to the next project."

"Which is?" she asks.

"I don't know, yet. I'll have to pull something from the idea file." For the first time in weeks, I don't have something to work on. That makes me panicky. Okay, beyond panicky. Finishing a draft feels like a relief, but it's really just a face-first kick into uncertainty.

When you finish something, you have to start something new.

"You should come with me," Sherri says, sipping her water. "When I go to Sundance."

"You think?" I've never been; I'm not a skier, and Utah has worked hard to make itself sound like the least interesting place in the United States in every other respect. But it's different now that my friend is going to be there, having an important career moment. I should definitely be there for that. "I mean, you wouldn't mind?"

"Why would I mind? You're my best friend, I'm going to need you there to slap me when I start acting like a big star." She frowns. "Unless you're needed here for rewrites or something."

"My only conflict might be if Dana decides to pick that week for wedding number three." My sister sometimes has impeccable timing. "And, if filming hasn't wrapped up by then, I'll probably have Jack's funeral or something. Otherwise, I'm golden."

"I heard casting started." Sherri wiggles her eyebrows. "For the big time parts."

We've already been through this. "Jason McEwan is not going to be starring. And I know that one guy, from the cop show, he's trying to whip up his fan club into a frenzy, but nothing is going to come of it." Jack already expressed his distaste at the public embarrassment the dude was making of himself chasing the role.

"No, I'm not talking about for Damian. I'm talking about Ella. Madison Avery is very, very high in the running, if the gossip can be believed." Sherri sips her water, then adds, "My agent said there would be sides coming my way, if you're interested."

"For Ella?" I hate to even think it, but there's no way Sherri is going to get a read for the role. They're looking for a barely legal ingénue.

They're looking for someone just like Madison Avery. Maybe that's why Jack was talking to her at the party.

Sherri shakes her head. "No, for something else. Damian's sister or something?"

"Oh, right." The character's main function in the novel is to be beaten up by her abusive boyfriend, so Damian can heroically rescue her. She didn't have a huge role on the page, and she'll probably have less of one on screen. "That's not a very big part, though."

"Beef her up a little!" Sherri jokes. "Seriously, though, getting into a movie like this, even as the maid with no lines? It wouldn't be bad for me."

"It would be a lateral move. Remember how you always say I'm so much better than this?" I remind her.

"You might be, but I'm not. I've got a limited shelf-life."

I don't bother to point out that if *Beautiful Darkness* flops, I'll be past my sell-by date, too.

\* \* \* \*

Prepared for the meeting like I'm going into battle, I step off the elevator and breeze past the huge brushed steel letters that spell out "Macrocosm" along the wall of the reception area.

"I'm here for Jack Martin," I tell the girl at the desk, but she's already expecting me.

"Go on back, I'll let him know you're coming."

For a massive movie studio, Macrocosm headquarters are surprisingly small and plain. The executive floor is basically a hallway to various offices and conference rooms. I've heard the studio heads have whole floors with their own lobbies, but I've never been up higher than the seventh story.

Despite his box office successes, Jack doesn't have one of those sacred floors. He does have a huge corner office, and that's where I head. The door is open, and his chair faces the windows. When I enter, he turns slowly, fingers steepled in front of him. With a tilt of his head, he says, "I'm sure you're wondering why I've gathered you all here today."

"That never gets olds," I say, in a tone of voice that indicates yes, it absolutely gets old, but I tolerate it only because it's him. "Where is everyone?"

"You're the first one here. Blew your power move." He gestures to the sitting area, where a couch and two chairs surround a coffee table. As I approach it, I see the top is covered with neat piles of headshots.

"Are you guys talking casting today?" I don't recognize the man on top of the pile for Damian Bennett. I recognize Ella, and I don't think to stop myself before uttering a relieved, "Oh…"

"Oh, what?" Jack steps up behind me and frowns down at my finger touching the glossy black-and-white photo of Madison Avery.

I jerk my hand back like he's caught me shoplifting. "Just 'oh'. As in, makes sense."

As in, makes sense why you were talking to her at the party. As in, makes no sense for me to feel the uncomfortable, heavy jealousy in my gut that I've been feeling ever since that night.

What Jack and I have is casual. That was what we agreed upon, so I have no right to be upset if he starts seeing someone. We have provisions in place for the friendly dissolution of our Dom/sub relationship. And while I spent that first Tuesday after the party pacing the floor, certain that he would come in and tell me that he'd fallen deeply in love with Madison, she didn't even come up. It took a lot out of me to get into the right mindset that night. I got over it—what man wouldn't want to spend time talking to a beautiful woman at a party? It meant nothing. But seeing her picture here, in his office, puts me back on the defensive.

It's stupid and pointless. Jack is terrible at romantic relationships. It's why he doesn't do them, ever. With one exception, I've never known him to have a partner, male or female, since we met. Horrible fiancé really messed him up. Romance just isn't something he's good at. And even if he was, it wouldn't matter. Our arrangement works for us, but change one or two things, and it's something neither of us would want. A partner on the side? Would change things. I would be sad to lose Jack as my sub, but I have no right to want him to stay lonely forever just so I can tie him up.

Jack's brow furrows critically as he stares down at the photo. "I don't know. I like Steph DeLuca. But nobody's read, yet. These are just the ones who got sides."

"Right." I sit on the sofa. I know where I rank in this meeting, and it's not a chair of my own.

"I've arrived," Lynn's voice announces from the doorway. She's followed by Kathy, who carries a huge bag. "I've just come from a meeting with my publisher. *Beautiful Lightness* is a go!"

I'm so glad I'm not drinking anything, because I would have spit it out.

"*Beautiful Lightness*?" Jack asks, his expression carefully blank. He deserves an Oscar for not laughing.

"Yes, it's a sequel," Lynn clarifies. "I can't go into much more detail, but suffice it to say, I am very, *very* happy this morning. My agent is hashing out the rest of the details."

The tension in Jack's shoulders increases visibly. Another book means another movie—if this one is a success. So much more is riding on us, now.

Before any of us can panic, Marion Cross breezes into the room. Marion is tall, made taller by the chunky high-heeled boots she wears. She's in her fifties, though you wouldn't know it for the dark drum-tight skin stretched over her elegant cheekbones. Her hair falls in waist-length braids down the back of her black leather jacket. She looks like a professional assassin from an Urban Fantasy book, not a director, but she has two Golden Globes and an Academy Award under her belt.

"Good afternoon, everyone," she says, smoothly taking command.

"Marion." Jack crosses to take her hand and give it a firm shake. "Good to see you."

"You, too, Jack." She leans in to kiss the air beside his cheek. They're almost the same height. Then, she turns to Lynn. "And I hear you've got some news."

"You did?" Lynn's gaze snaps to Kathy, her expression frosty. "I wonder how."

Marion gestures over her shoulder. "I was in the hallway. I overheard you."

"Right, well, let's just close the door, then." Jack does just that then joins us around the table. Marion sits beside me on the sofa, and Lynn sighs.

"Something wrong?" Kathy asks, instantly rummaging through the bag she carries.

"There's nowhere for you to sit." Lynn looks at me pointedly, and I realize two things. The most obvious that she wants me to stand for the meeting so her assistant can sit. The less obvious to anyone but me? She's read the screenplay. And she's not happy.

"Sorry, Kathy," Jack says, gallantly retrieving a chair from in front of his desk.

"You have a bigger office than Keith Thompson," Marion says with a laugh.

"I've earned this studio more money than Keith Thompson has," Jack deadpans, and that only makes Marion laugh more.

Then, as if noticing me for the first time, she points at me and says, "You're the scribe."

I have never heard anyone use the word "scribe" in a non-ironic context before. I think I'm in love.

"Yeah, that's me."

"I love what you did with it," Marion says, and I know instantly that she's the kind of person who doesn't give empty compliments.

"We are going to discuss the script today, right?" Lynn asks Jack. She turns to me and says, "I admire some of what you did, but I feel it's absolutely necessary that I be involved in the rewrite."

"I anticipated that," I tell her pleasantly. And I did assume she would be involved, as well as Jack and Marion.

"What, exactly, do you think needs to be changed?" Somehow, Marion's question is an undeniable challenge without being confrontational enough to spark an argument.

Lynn has to respond civilly, and she knows it. "Well, there are still some issues with how beta Damian is turning out."

"I think he's softened," Jack interjects. "But I don't see that as a bad thing."

Marion agrees with an emphatic nod.

Lynn laughs. "Oh, so we're going to talk about this, now?"

"We have to start somewhere." Jack's smile is disingenuous and frozen. "What would you like to discuss first?"

"Casting." She folds her arms. "Who do we have for Damian?"

"Paula has sent sides to a few people." Jack introduces the head-shots one-by-one, naming each actor and briefing us on his positives and negatives.

"I haven't heard of any of these people," Lynn says, looking over the photos critically. "They're very good-looking, but none of them are stars."

"People aren't going to come to this movie to see stars," Marion explains. "I want unknowns, so viewers aren't distracted. There are going to be some pretty intense scenes, and we don't want them thinking, *this is what this actor looks like having sex.*"

"Right," Jack agrees. "The movie is going to be big enough that we don't need big names to draw them in."

I almost laugh, but thankfully keep it bottled up. It's not that we don't *need* big stars. It's that the actors up for consideration will take a much smaller paycheck, increasing the profit margins. Jack and Marion are right; the movie will sell itself, no matter who's in it.

"Well, wait," Marion says, leaning forward to scoop Madison Avery's photo and résumé off the top. "Then, why are we considering her?"

Jack frowns. "She's not what I would call a star."

"She was on the cover of *People* two months ago. She's not 'unknown' if she's on one of the biggest shows on TV." Marion lets the photo fall back onto the pile.

Jack picks it up. "On TV. She hasn't had any major film roles, yet. Unless you're going to count," he traces down the page with his finger, "when she played the daughter in *Stolen*."

"And she was only in that for ten minutes," Kathy pipes up. One look from Lynn silences her.

"That's a good point," Marion says, and I'm pierced with the strangest sense of betrayal. But Marion hasn't done anything to betray me.

God, I'm jealous of Madison Avery. I'm jealous of a woman in her twenties, who I see as a threat to my non-relationship with a forty-year-old who flirted with her at a party. If it were any other forty-year-old, I would probably roll my eyes at him.

For the rest of the meeting, I avoid eye contact with Madison Avery's headshot. We go over the list of actresses, but the whole time, I have a sick feeling in my gut. She's perfect for the part. She hasn't read for it, yet, but there's no one else I can imagine in the role.

"We'll follow up on this when Paula gets back to us," Jack says, then focuses on Lynn. "Now, these are all the people who received sides. Not the people who'll necessarily read. Some of them might not be interested."

"Because of the script?" she asks.

Marion blinks at her. Jack is speechless. I hold my breath.

When Jack does speak, his tone is frosty. "No. Not because of the script."

"They've only received a few scenes from it, anyway." Why does my voice sound so small and uncertain? Marion intimidates me, the same way I was intimidated by Jack when we first started working together. No matter how much experience I have, they both definitely have more. But why am I terrified of Lynn? I decide not to let that happen, again. With more confidence, I remind her, "As per your request for secrecy, no one is going to be able to leak a full script and ruin things for your fans."

"Well, that's a relief. Because the screenplay I read is not the book I wrote."

There it is.

The silence in the room makes the three of us far more uncomfortable than it does Lynn. Even Kathy retreats to intense concentration centered on her phone.

Jack seems unsure how proceed, so he does so cautiously, like a man avoiding quicksand. "Maybe we should start with the big items and work our way down to more specific details?"

"For one, there's dialogue in the script that can't be found anywhere in my book," Lynn says. Her gaze skates over me as she looks from Jack to Marion. I might as well not even be in the room. "Kathy can tell you, I was up until four in the morning doing a side-by-side comparison. I was heartsick."

*Heartsick?*

"Is there a reason for the changes," Jack asks me. I know I'm not on trial—Jack is asking so I can offer an explanation without seeming defensive or aggressive—but I still feel like I'm about to be cross-examined.

"There were a few instances where I felt internal monologues had important points that we'd lose on the screen." That was true; nothing I added hadn't been in Lynn's book.

"Which isn't uncommon," Marion is quick to inform Lynn.

"But some of the dialogue was changed," Lynn protests. "The dialogue *I* wrote, I mean. The real dialogue. Ella never speaks with contractions, and this script is just peppered with them."

She's right. Ella never spoke with contractions in the novel. It made all of her lines either robotic or archaic sounding. That's why I added them back in.

"People are used to hearing—and speaking—in contractions," I tell her.

"Ella Vaughn isn't 'most people'," Lynn says with a little laugh, as though the character is a real human being I woefully underestimated. "She speaks the way she does because she was an English major, and she's obsessed with Jane Austen."

"I don't know," Marion interjects. "I've read everything Austen ever wrote, and I still use contractions."

"It's an integral part of her character," Lynn insists.

"It's going to be difficult for an actress to deliver, 'I do not,' and 'I cannot' without sounding like she's stepping out of a period piece," Jack says, and I know right away that this is a battle I'm going to win. Jack might not act as much, anymore, but he'll never lose touch with those roots.

Lynn narrows her eyes. "Then, I would suggest hiring a decent actress."

"Let's move on," Marion says, steering us away from a nasty conflict. "What other problems do you have?"

"The scene, the 'aftercare' as you put it," Lynn says, addressing me. "It's still in there, when I made it very clear that it would be removed."

Before I can respond, Marion says, "Oh, I liked that part. I thought it softened Damian up a lot."

"Damian isn't soft!" Lynn barks.

The room goes silent. I've been present for some heated throw-downs in rooms just like these, but never has anyone sounded so shrill and despotic before.

With a little more composure, she goes on. "My readers like Damian because he is alpha. An alpha hero despises weakness."

"I don't think taking care of someone you're supposed to love is a weakness," I snap back. I know immediately that I've used the wrong words.

"Are you suggesting that Damian doesn't love Ella?" Lynn asks, incredulous. "Because millions—and I mean over one-hundred million—readers disagree with you."

"Okay, okay," Jack says, scrubbing a hand over his mouth. "Marion. What are your thoughts on the scene?"

She shrugs. "I said I liked it. It fills in a gap left by the removal of Ella's inner monologue."

Hearing my own reasoning for the inclusion of the scene roll off someone else's tongue like it's the most obvious thing in the world? I want to throw a victorious fist in the air.

"Well, I have final approval over the script, so we'll just see, shall we?" Lynn says with chipper malice.

"Lynn…" Jack begins, leaning forward in his chair. He braces his elbows on his thighs and hangs his hands between them. "You've got final approval; nobody is challenging that. But films are a collaborative effort. We're all doing what we can to make your book look good on screen."

"I appreciate that," she says, giving Jack a smile that I doubt Marion or I will ever see. "And you're very patient with me as I learn the ins and outs here. I know you all have more experience, but I have far more experience as a novelist—"

"I've written two novels," Marion corrects her.

Lynn tilts her head and gives Marion a pinched, polite expression. "Then, you understand why I'm so protective over mine. I don't think you can compare 'I've written two novels' to writing one of the most acclaimed and bestselling books of all time."

I almost need to be physically restrained to keep from interjecting, "Half-right!" *Beautiful Darkness* might be the biggest bestseller of all time, but it's far from the most acclaimed novel in history.

Marion doesn't let a drop of Lynn's ego splash on her. "Maybe you're right. Maybe you can't compare the two. But I do have an Oscar. That should count for something."

She might as well have dropped the little gold man like a microphone.

Lynn stands abruptly. "Well, this has been quite a meeting. But I have something on my schedule, don't I, Kathy?"

Kathy looks frantically through her phone. "Y-yes. You have…an appointment."

Kathy is a terrible liar.

Nobody is going to call Lynn on her brush-off, though. I think everyone in the room wants the meeting to be over.

"We'll pick up on this another time," Jack says, standing to shake Lynn's hand.

She puts on her sunglasses, instead, and leaves Jack hanging. "Yes, we'll be in touch. Maybe it would be more effective if our next meeting wasn't so crowded."

Kathy frantically collects all of her things and scurries after her through the door. Lynn's voice is loud enough that we can hear her all the way down the hall. I don't try to make out what she's saying.

"That was a nice preview," Marion says with a sharp exhale of disbelief. "Has she been like this the whole time?"

"No. We've just had a steady escalation," Jack says grimly.

"Approval or no approval, we've got to keep these characters from coming across as a medieval princess and a deranged psychopath," she goes on. "You better have my back on this. I'm doing this as a favor to Macrocosm, not you."

Oh, that's an interesting development.

"I know, I know." Jack leans back in his chair and covers his face with both hands. "And I've got your back."

"We just have to figure out a way to have each others' backs behind hers," I tell them.

Jack sits upright again, blinking like a man just waking up. "Why couldn't this just be a straightforward adaptation?"

"Because someone at this studio had a gas leak in their office during negotiations?" Marion shrugs. "Who gives a first-time author this much creative control?"

"Too late to cry over that, now," Jack reminds us both. "Look, I've got to get to the gym before my three o'clock. Let's all just take twenty-four hours to cool down and figure out how to proceed, before I call Lynn and start kissing ass to make up for all of this."

"Fine by me." I stand and pull my keys from the pocket of my laptop bag. "I'll just be waiting for revisions, then."

I won't really be waiting by the inbox or anything. There's always the next script to work on.

*Or your book*, my conscience nags me. *If Marion can write her novels and win an Oscar, you can finish yours.*

"Sounds good. I'll be in touch," Marion says, following me to the door. I notice she didn't tell Jack to stay in touch. Marion Cross is the kind of person who contacts you. You don't contact Marion Cross.

In the hallway, she asks, "Jessica? Can I have a word?"

She can have several. I'm so in awe of her talent and her confidence, I feel like God has shone a spotlight on me.

"I've dealt with people like Lynn Baldwin before," Marion says, her voice low. "She's not going to be happy unless she writes, directs, and stars in the damn thing herself."

A short sharp laugh escapes me. How many times have I thought the exact same thing?

"Sorry for that mental image," Marion adds. "Don't let her get to you. I'm on your side, here. Jack is on your side. We're going to have to make the best of it."

"That's what I don't understand," I say with a shake of my head. "If nobody working on this actually likes it, what's the point?"

"It's the biggest book of all time. Someone was going to make this movie, and make a killing. It might as well be us."

Marion has a point. If Macrocosm hadn't bought the movie, someone else would be making it. I wouldn't be getting paid to write it. Marion wouldn't be getting paid to direct it. Jack wouldn't be producing it.

Jack wouldn't be producing it and considering Madison Avery for the part.

Jack wouldn't be considering Madison Avery.

I have to keep that thought far, far from my mind.

Jenny Trout

April 24, 2009

"I can't believe it," I say for what has to be the twenty-thousandth time on this journey. I've had these moments of disbelief at least once a day since I got the call that Macrocosm wanted to buy my screenplay.

And none of it would have happened without Jack.

He loops an arm companionably around my shoulders, and my heart flutters.

Those moments have been coming pretty often, too.

"Believe it," he says, taking a swig from his beer bottle. "And it's my turn to say 'I can't believe it.' You've gotten to do that enough."

"Oh, please, like you haven't done a thousand movies." I roll my eyes and scan the soundstage. There are so many people here. Cast members who finished shooting weeks ago, camera men and boom operators who've only just finished stowing their equipment. I've never seen a wrap party before. It's nothing like the cast parties I remember from doing theatre in college. Everyone is way more laid back than they were just hours before when Jack called out, "That's a wrap!"

Principle shooting is finished. For my movie. Not my screenplay. My *movie*. It's something completely different, now, totally out of my control. The actors spoke my words. The director and cinematographer staged my scenes. So many people worked on *Still Waters* that it isn't even mine, anymore. It just is. It exists with or without me, now.

My stomach sours

"Are you okay?" Jack asks immediately, and I realize that the shoulders he still rests his arm on are painfully tense.

I shrug him off. "Yeah. It's like I suddenly realized that my words are in a movie."

"I know how you feel." When I laugh, he says, "No, seriously. This is the first time I've directed anything. You think I'm not nervous now that there's no take-backs?"

"How do you do it, then?" I ask, marveling at how easy everyone else seems to be taking it. "You have to have some tips for this kind of thing."

"As a matter of fact…" He reaches into his shirt pocket and produces a joint. "This helps a lot."

"You're not supposed to have that here," I remind him. "We're on set. Only doctor prescribed pharmaceutical tranquilizers allowed, for health and safety reasons."

He chuckles. "Then, let's not get caught. Come on."

He offers me his hand, and I glance at the cast and crew swarming the craft services table and hugging like it's the last day of summer camp.

Yeah, I have to get out of here. Half of these people have never even met me in person.

"I don't know why I even came," I tell Jack. "I feel so out-of-place."

"Here's a secret," he says, pushing open the door of the sprawling soundstage. He squints against the sunlight. "And you can't tell anybody I told you this. But not a damn person in this town feels like they're supposed to be here."

"Bob Ardsman," I counter, citing one of the most confident, self-assured people I'd met in L.A. He declined to represent me at ICW, but he practically forced my agent to take me on, instead.

Jack grimaces. "Okay, you got me there. Exception that proves the rule, okay?"

"Fine." I laugh as we round the building and slip behind a row of construction dumpsters. It feels like I'm a teenager, again, trying to be sneaky. I look nervously in both directions as he sparks up the joint.

"Relax," he says in that tight-chest, breath-holding voice. He blows blue-tinged smoke from his mouth and adds, "Do you know how much money I make for this studio? What are they gonna do to me?"

"Spank you?" I suggest, taking the joint from him.

He sputters a laugh. He has no idea, yet, that I left my side job two weeks ago. Not because I'm rolling in that mad Hollywood cash, but because it took up too much time. I've gotten this far; I can't let it all slip away, now, just because there's a more secure paycheck in the rut I just left.

That doesn't mean I don't miss it, though.

I pass the weed back to him. In the cool-tinged light of the alley, Jack looks like he could be in a movie, right now. His hazel eyes fix on me, and he tilts his head as he takes another hit. Smoke curling from his lips, he asks, "Is this collaboration…you and me, working together…is it temporary?"

I want to ask him who he thinks I'm going to work with, instead. He plucked me from obscurity, as the saying goes. He's the one who made all of this happen for me, just by believing in me. And working with him is fun. Sometimes. We definitely had our disagreements, but the fact that I even feel comfortable disagreeing with him when he's Jack freaking Martin is a testament to how dedicated he is to the craft and not his ego.

There's a lot I admire about Jack. He's no longer a larger-than-life movie star figure to me. He's my mentor—as weird as that is to say about someone who's only a year older than you.

"No, it's not temporary," I say, then add, "not unless you want it to be."

"I don't want it to be." He shakes his head. "But what I want…"

"What?" I nudge him. He can't hide internal conflict. He's a good actor, but a terrible liar.

"I don't want any of this to be temporary." He flicks the joint aside like it's a cigarette. "I don't want *you* to be temporary."

I don't know how it happens. One second we're having one of our usual casually deep interactions, the ones that provide an outlet while saving us from revealing too much to each other. From revealing too much to anyone, because neither of us can stand that vulnerability. And in the next breath, we're both totally vulnerable, as he takes my face in his hands and kisses me the way…

Well, the way people do in movies, as the saying goes.

The worst—best?—part is that I kiss him back. I'm ruining my career before it gets off the ground. I'm making a huge mistake doing this with a guy who's basically my boss. I'm risking everything I've worked for.

But I don't stop kissing him. Not even when he backs me against the wall, and I can't decide which is harder, the brick or the body pinning me to it. His lips are softer than I imagined they would be. Wait, I imagined this? Maybe a hundred times, a thousand times, without knowing.

He lifts his mouth and whispers, his voice ragged and pleading, "I don't just want to fuck you—"

My knees go weak at the word.

"—I want to be with you."

And our hands are on each other, again. Without realizing it, somewhere during our collaboration, this happened to us. Maybe I wouldn't have realized it if he didn't make the first move. Everything was so busy and shiny and new, it distracted me.

Somehow, I missed it when I fell in love with him.

We leave the lot without saying goodbye to anyone at the party. It's probably poor form, but we're so drunk on each other that we can't make good choices. He drives us to that hillside mansion that I used to find so intimidating, but that I now just think of as Jack's house, and we barely talk on the way. His hands shake as he punches in the security code. They shake more when we're inside and he's peeling off my blouse.

He pushes my hips against the wall, right there in the foyer, and holds me that way. His mouth slides down my neck, to my shoulder, to the tops of my breasts with their goose-bumped skin.

I reach between us to pop the buttons on his shirt. In a moment of impulsiveness, I just rip them apart. He laughs against my chest and boosts me up to wrap my legs around his waist. Staggering a little, he manages to take us down the two steps from the foyer, into the living room. We tumble onto a wide soft black leather couch, and he rises over me with one knee between my thighs.

"We're doing this, then?" he asks, his eyes desperately scanning mine, like he's looking for a promise, instead of an answer.

"Yes." My chest is tight. "All of it."

And I mean it.

## Chapter Six

"Big news from the set of *Beautiful Darkness*," the Entertainment Channel anchor bleats cheerfully. His face is just slightly too tan, his teeth just slightly too tall and white. His hair wouldn't move in a wind tunnel, and the shape of it probably makes him aerodynamic.

He's actually a really nice guy. I'm just being pissy, because I know what he's going to say. I snap the button on the remote and toss it onto the table.

"Super cute and amazing actress Madison Avery will be baring every inch of her unblemished twenty-year-old body as the new star of *Beautiful Darkness*," I say to my empty living room. Which is a shame, because I do a great impression of Too-Tan McToothy on TV.

There is no reason for me to be upset about the casting of Madison Avery. She's perfect for the role, just "unknown" enough that she can bring the movie a fresh wave of hype, and she's genuinely humble and gracious. But every time I think of her, I think of Jack's body language at the party. The way he stood just a little closer to her than he would anyone else.

He used to stand next to me that way.

I make a frustrated noise at myself and check the time on my phone. My car will be arriving any minute, and here I am, mooning over the past. And it's totally unwarranted. Jack hasn't shown any indication that he's even remotely interested in her, and he and I aren't remotely interested in getting back together. Any insecurity I feel is probably just to do with this stupid movie and the woman who opposes every move anyone makes.

My phone vibrates on the coffee table, and I pick it up. It's Jack. I frown as I slide my thumb across the screen. "Yeah?"

"Just calling to wish you a happy flight," he says, sounding way too smug about the fact that he's sending me across the country with *that* woman.

It's how I've started to think of Lynn Baldwin in my head. *That* woman. It's a nice counterpoint to her always referring to me as "she", as though I'm not in the room.

"I'll be happier when it's the return flight." I glance at my laptop case. "You might not realize it, but screenwriters *can* be busy. I'm in the middle of a draft for that firefighter movie, and Ari wants to see it by next Monday."

"I appreciate you taking so much time away for this." Damn it, he sounds sincere, so I can't be pissed at him. "It's only an overnight trip. There and back."

"On a cross-country flight," I remind him. "And we get to sit on a panel and smile and pretend we all get along."

"You get along with Marion," he says then swears. He must be calling from the car. "Sorry, some guy just cut me off."

"Does she have any complaints about the nine-hundredth rewrite, or is she planning on springing her notes on me when I get to the con?" I want to know before I go in. My biggest hope for the trip is that we only see each other at the panel.

"I haven't received any notes from her. I also told her to relax and enjoy the convention, and not worry about business while she's there." Though I can't see Jack, I know he's grimacing, just from the tone of his voice and the brief pause after his words. "We'll see how that goes."

"Well, I got your debriefing email, and I've been practicing saying, 'It's been a pleasure working with Lynn,' without it sounding like an obvious lie, so I think I'm ready." A horn beeps outside, and I curse. "That's my ride. I have to go."

"I'll check in later. Try not to rip Lynn's hair out by the roots?" he implores.

I laugh. "I can't promise that."

"Then, do it where nobody can get video. I'll talk to you later."

We hang up, and I grab my laptop bag and hard-sided carry-on. I don't do checked luggage. Then, I set the alarm, lock the door, and head out to the waiting black car.

If it were any other movie, or really, any other author, I would be psyched about appearing at a convention and sitting on a panel. I've only done it twice before, and those were stuffy film festival events. The Romantic Nights convention sounds like an event people go to for fun, and it probably would be fun for me, if I weren't going there specifically to talk about *Beautiful Darkness.*

Maybe I'll get some free books out of the deal.

On the ride to the airport, my phone chimes with a new email. It's from my sub, asking, *Tuesday, Mistress?*

*Tuesday,* I confirm, then quickly follow with, *And you're not allowed to cum until then. No cheating. I'll know.*

Something about that itches at the back of my brain. It's not unusual for me to order him to abstain. But a growing discomfort nags at me. Did I ask him to do this as part of his submission? Or did I ask him to do it because I'm afraid he'll sleep with someone? It would be a gross abuse of our relationship if the latter were the case.

The fact that I don't know if I'm capable of doing something so low is reason enough for Jack and I to have a real talk when I get back.

****

The Romantic Nights convention is held in a different city every year. Last year, it was in San Diego. That would have been a way better commute than L.A. to Atlanta. By the time I get off the plane, my legs don't seem to work properly and my face feels dryer than sandpaper in Las Vegas. I take out my Evian spray and spritz myself in the bathroom before I head down to the car that's waiting for me.

The hotel is in downtown Atlanta and is, I'm informed by my chatty driver, one of the venues for a popular science fiction convention.

"You're from L.A., you probably know all the stars that come through here. The main guys from *Supernatural*—my wife loves the show—the *Walking Dead* guys, I drove all of them," he tells me as we inch down the congested highway. "And you know that lady, the one who wrote that smutty book? I drove her yesterday."

My stomach churns, both at his description of the book and the idea that Lynn has already arrived.

By the time I get to the hotel, I'm exhausted. The heat in Atlanta is nothing like the heat back home. At least, there, it doesn't feel like someone's just thrown at bucket of warm water over me every time I step outside. I practically collapse on the check-in counter while the woman at the desk types at lightning speed.

Also like lightning? The flashes coming from the bar area far across the lobby. I squint toward the commotion happening.

"It's Lynn Baldwin," the woman behind the counter says, sliding my ID back to me. "She is so nice. She's been down here taking pictures with people for two hours, now."

"You don't say." So nice, my ass. She's not doing anything for her fans. She's there to feed her ego.

"I just love her book," the woman goes on. She slips some key cards into an envelope. "Here are your keys and your room number. The elevators are going to be around the corner here."

"Thank you," I mumble and leave as quickly as possible.

\*\*\*\*

Our panel the next morning is in the grand ballroom, but despite the seating capacity, it's still standing room only. It's hot and packed, and Lynn enters to deafening applause. The heat in the space, combined with the noise and the uncomfortable night I spent getting dehydrated by the air conditioner, makes me feel about as bad as I suspect I look. For some reason—insecurity, most likely—I thought I should go for a dressed-down, L.A. chic look. One of those, "Oh, I just ran out for a gallon of milk in these deconstructed jeans and classic white tee," outfits.

Except celebrities actually had those jeans and t-shirts tailored to make them look that damn good. That was a secret I learned from Jack. I forgot that when I was getting dressed this morning, and now, I look like I just rolled in from painting a house.

Meanwhile, Lynn is decked out smartly in a black pantsuit over a turquoise v-neck silk shell. Her diamond ring throws a disco ball pattern on the tabletop, and her hair is immaculately pulled up in a French twist.

This is a side of Lynn I've never seen. She's usually casual, but carefully staged, like a Food Network host. Now, she appears more polished, more professional.

Beside her, Marion shows us both up in bootcut jeans, Converse sneakers, and a long ribbed knit tunic. Everything about her wardrobe is understated; she doesn't need anything to make her look like she's playing a part. She is exactly as cool as she looks.

"Good morning, good morning!" A chipper dark-haired woman warbles into a microphone. She's probably in her mid-forties and has the tan skin and accent of someone who's lived in the area for a long time. "I'm Patty Turner, I'm your panel moderator—"

Polite applause and a few isolated "Whoo!"s filter up to us. Patty pauses for a bashful smile and laugh. Her name was on an ad that wrapped the elevator doors. She must be a novelist in her own right.

I wonder what kind of pull she has, that she's gotten this opportunity. How does she feel about introducing another, more famous writer? Is she grateful to share the spotlight with her, even for forty-five minutes? Is she humbled or embarrassed? I can't imagine Lynn cheerfully playing second fiddle to a more famous author.

"It looks like everyone in the hotel is here," Patty quips.

"Except the haters!" someone shouts from the crowd.

Lynn leans toward her microphone and says slyly, "Well, we don't need them, anyway."

And she doesn't. Lynn Baldwin doesn't need even half of her readers to be an overwhelming success. Yet, her fans seem obsessed with the "haters", reviewers and readers who don't care for the book and make their critiques—and sometimes, vitriol—known. Somehow, they believe that even a single dissenting opinion endangers Lynn's career.

After the scene I witnessed in the lobby last night, I looked up some of the message boards and fansites that have cropped up in celebration of *Beautiful Darkness.* Facebook, for example, boasts no fewer than three hundred fan groups devoted not just to Lynn, but to individual characters and even inanimate objects like Damian Bennett's helicopter, Whiskey Tango Foxtrot. Her fans roleplay, write fan fiction, and create artwork, but they seem dedicated, over all else, to combating "haters". To them, Lynn is still the suburban everywoman, and they'll protect her and her book at all costs.

The internet is a strange place.

Knowing that even the mildest criticism can get one branded a "hater" terrifies me, especially now that I'm in a room with so many fans. I feel like I'm on a spy mission into enemy territory. But it will be useful. Here, I'll figure out what readers are really looking for, and hopefully, I'll be able to use some of that as we continue to argue over rewrites.

"Since we already know who Lynn is, we can save her introduction for last," Patty says, and gestures to Marion. "How about you introduce yourself?"

Marion leans toward her mic. "I'm Marion Cross, and I'm directing *Beautiful Darkness,* the movie."

"I'm Jessica Yates," I say on my turn. "I wrote the screenplay for *Beautiful Darkness.*"

"So, if there's anything you don't like, she's the one to complain to," Lynn adds. She laughs when she says it, like it's a clever joke, but my guts churn.

*It must be nice to have someone to blame if your shitty book becomes a shitty movie,* I snarl internally, but force myself to laugh it off.

"And of course, I'm Lynn—"

Her last name is lost to a roar of excitement from the audience. She waits for it to subside before adding, "And I wrote *Beautiful Darkness*."

The moderator lets the applause escalate to thunder before she quiets everyone over her own mic. "Okay, okay. Let's ask her some questions, rather than just shout at her."

All of the questions are fairly basic. How did Lynn handle her sudden fame? How did she manage to write a whole book while caring for her husband and children? Did she have any tips for writers who are just starting out?

One woman in the crowd blushes and stammers, "Damian and Ella are so real. What inspired them? Where did they come from?"

A few murmurs of agreement ripple through the crowd.

Lynn smiles and says, "They came from me."

This takes me aback. I've heard and read writers answering this question before, and the response is almost always that they were based on people in real life, or they came to the writer in a dream. Sometimes, "the muse" gets the credit.

"And it was damned hard work," she adds, to the room's delight. "I knew I had a story to tell, but until I sat down and really put pen to paper, brainstorming ideas and stuff, I didn't have anything. I had to build these characters and this world from the ground up. Anyone who tells you there's an easier way is selling you something."

I'm struck by the profoundness of her statement, and her ability to accept the praise without downplaying the effort she invested. For all that Lynn is brand-new to this, she at least has a handle on one of the most important aspects of being a woman writer. She won't let her light be smothered under a bushel of societally-imposed modesty.

The next question concerns the movie, specifically how explicit the famed sex will be. Marion describes her vision for sensual, but not pornographic, love scenes. "We don't want the sex to be the only thing they talk about," she says, though both of us—hell, everyone in the room—knows that's unavoidable.

"We've trimmed a few scenes here and there, for the same reason," I add. "A lot of factors come into play when you get into distribution and the MPAA—"

"Though I'm sure it wouldn't hurt us to get slapped with an NC-17," Lynn interrupts, drawing laughs from the audience. Before I can continue, she goes on. "But the script isn't finalized, yet. As our wonderful producer often reminds me, nothing is final until the film ships."

That's not only false, it's also a dangerous illusion to foster in a known control freak. My guess is that Jack resorted to telling her that as a way to distract her from an objection he didn't want to discuss, but it wasn't smart of him.

The next person to ask a question doesn't look nervous or star struck at all. She wears a retro-cut dress printed like scribbled-on parchment and holds a notebook. Her pen is poised above the paper. "I'd like to address an earlier answer you gave, Ms. Baldwin. You said that your only inspiration for the characters of Ella and Damian came from your own head?"

For no discernable reason, Lynn's face tightens into that smiling mask of anger I've grown painfully used to. "No, no. I said the characters came from my brain. I don't think I've made any secret of the fact that our wonderful producer, Jack Martin, was the physical inspiration for Damian."

I'm going to tease Jack mercilessly—the nonsexual version of teasing, anyway—when we talk next. If Lynn keeps referring to him that way, I'm going to demand he credit himself as "Wonderful Producer Jack Martin".

"Will he be in the movie?" someone shouts, and the moderator hushes her, saying, "Let's all wait our turns."

The woman in the parchment dress is still standing, not satisfied with Lynn's response. "That's what I want to discuss. Fans of Martin's movie *Last Man Standing* have noted similarities between *Beautiful Darkness* and a popular fan fiction based on that movie."

"If there are similarities, they're certainly coincidental." Lynn is openly frosty, now, though I can't blame her. It sounds a lot like she's being called a plagiarist, in front of hundreds of fans. "After all," she continues, "there are no new ideas. To every author's lament."

"Let's take another one," the moderator tries, but the questioner raises her voice to speak over her.

"Plagiarism detecting software noted that seventy percent of *Beautiful Darkness* is identical to the fic, 'Darkness Standing', and readers and reviewers have found the plot and characterization identical."

"Sit down!" someone shouts, and a few people cheer and clap.

"This isn't a discussion I'd like to have at this time," Lynn says, staring past the woman.

I follow her gaze and see two women in t-shirts emblazoned with "STAFF" coming down the aisle toward the questioner.

Lynn continues, "If you would contact my publicist, I'll be happy to discuss this issue further."

"Your publicist won't return my emails," the woman shoots back impatiently. One of the staff members taps her on the shoulder. She collects her bags and, without a further scene, leaves. A smattering of applause and boos follows her.

"Okay, let's get back to the movie," the moderator says, her voice unsure. "Will Jack Martin be in the cast?"

"Oh, heavens, no!" Lynn brightens up, smoothly glossing past the incident. "No, he has a much more important role."

And like that, the plagiarism accusation is forgotten. But a new dread takes up residence in my stomach, alongside all the others in my growing collection of anxieties.

**\*\*\*\***

My flight is delayed two hours.

I roll my head on my stiff neck. The Atlanta humidity has bonded my makeup to my face on a molecular level. The security lines were almost as congested as the highway, so I raced to my gate in a panic, only to find that I'm just going to be sitting on my ass, again.

I swipe my thumb across my phone screen and check my texts. Nothing in L.A. gets done without a phone call. It's the most irritating thing in the world. But Jack knows how much I hate talking on the phone, so he's nice enough to text me.

*What happened?*

I frown. How could he have heard about the panel so quickly?

Opening twitter, I search the trending hashtags. Nothing, thank god. Then, I enter *Beautiful Darkness* into the search bar, and all hell breaks loose. The hashtag is a full-on battle between fans and haters, the latter of whom have broken the story of the plagiarism panel question and are out for blood.

I open my browser and look up "Darkness Standing", the fanfic the questioner had mentioned. I find it on a fanfiction site, and there it was, staring at me face-to-face.

*Darkness Standing by MollyCuddles94*

*Last Man Standing*

*No Warnings Tagged, Ben/Emma, hurt/comfort, dirty talk, Dom/sub, oral sex, vaginal sex, BDSM, spanking, smut*

My eyebrows lift at the last tag. It seems like that would be obvious.

*After his time in the military, Ben Jameson has built a fortune in business, but still feels the battle wounds in his heart. Reporter Emma Grace meets Ben while covering an underground fighting ring. Will their love be enough to heal them both?*

I frown at the summary. While the writing is clumsy, just replacing "Ben Jameson" and "Emma Grace" with "Damian Bennet" and "Ella Vaughn" makes it a spot-on description of *Beautiful Darkness*.

There are forty-six *thousand* comments.

I quickly close the application. This isn't a crisis I can deal with in an airport, and it's not even my crisis to begin with. This is something the studio—and, unfortunately, Jack—are going to have to deal with.

A flicker on the overhead television catches my eye. It's the Entertainment Channel, and Too-Tan McToothy is saying something I can't hear, because it's muted. The closed captions take some time to catch up with him, so the picture switches to footage of a red carpet and the words "HOT NEW ROMANCE?" pop up in all block print capitals. I ignore the rest of the text on the screen, because there, standing against a red-carpet photo backdrop is Madison Avery, and beside her is Jack, with his arm around her waist.

My face burns. I could acid wash jeans in my stomach, it's so sour. I open Jack's text again, trying to think of all the ways I could ask him about this.

I settle on replying to his earlier question with, *You tell me.*

February 19, 2011

I sit in my car for a full minute, my hands clenched on the steering wheel. I'm parked in Jack's driveway, and the gate has closed behind me. I feel trapped. Not by the gate, or by the rare heavy rain I'm not really trying to wait out.

He knows I'm here, sitting in my car. He's waiting for me to come in, and I can't.

I stare at the door, willing myself to move. Then, he's there, a darkened shape in the frosted glass pane. He opens the door and steps out. He hasn't shaved, so his lantern jaw is shadowed. He's wearing a gray t-shirt and dark jeans. In that moment, he looks better than I've ever seen him look, and I know it's because I can't keep him.

He's laughing as he dashes toward the car, and I unlock the door just as he reaches it.

"Waiting so you don't get wet?" he asks with a grin as he slides into the seat. "From the rain, I mean."

I have to say it, now. A moment longer and I'll lose my resolve. "We have to talk about something."

Doubt freezes, then gradually thaws his features. I can read what's going on in his head. Am I breaking up with him, or am I pregnant? Either would be his worst fear, but I can't spare him the truth.

"I can't be with you, anymore." Though I knew they were coming—I'm the one who said them—they sock me in the gut harder than any elbow I ever took playing girls' high school basketball.

His jaw tightens. He looks away, out the rain-spattered windshield. It's every breakup scene in every movie ever. But there's not going to be a resolution where we come together and work things out in the next scene. There can't be.

"Why?" he asks, clearing his throat and squinting beneath his rumpled brow.

"It's just that…" I know what I rehearsed in my head on the way over, but now, I hear it for the pathetic excuse that it is. "I need to focus on my career, right now."

"Yeah, and you can't do that dating me?" He rolls his eyes and makes a rough noise under his breath.

"I can't." In this, I have to be off-script and fully honest. "I mean, I can. But not without always wondering."

"What?" He's angry with me, and I don't blame him. I've unfairly blindsided him; I never even warned him that we needed to talk. "Without wondering what?"

I take a deep breath. We've talked about this before, but I don't want to give him the impression that this is a temporary fight or a discussion to fix things. "Without wondering if my work is what's selling, or if it's my access to you."

He sits back, blinking and frowning. "Wow. Okay. So, we're doing this, again."

"Don't." I blow out a breath in frustration. This conversation is tiresome and has been ever since we first had it. "You know what that *Vanity Fair* profile said. And you know what other people are saying. Look, I would love to be able to convince everyone that I'm getting by on my own merit. But I never had a chance. I've been Jack Martin's project, Jack Martin's writer, Jack Martin's girlfriend… I've never gotten to be Jessica Yates. I've come too far—"

"And who got you here, huh?" The words are violent and ugly because they're true. "You've never gotten to be Jessica Yates? Well boo-fucking-hoo. Who were you gonna be? Jasmine the stripper? Mistress Natasha?"

He's never thrown my past in my face before. Not once.

"I'm letting that slide because I know you're hurt, and you don't really mean it. But that's the only time you get to do that," I warn him. I'm not ashamed of my former line of work, and he knows that.

He doesn't apologize, but regret is written all over his face. After a long silence, he says, "There aren't many people in this town who get to be themselves. And good luck becoming a self-made man here."

"I'm not trying to be a self-made man," I grind out. "I'm trying to get out from under your name."

"My name got you the career you're leaving me for."

"Your name opened the door. I showed myself in." *That's a good line. I should remember that.*

"You know, a lot of people have tried to take advantage of me over the years, but I didn't expect it from you."

"I wasn't taking advantage of you!" I raise my voice in self-defense, but it's stupid of me. I'm not the one who just got their heart broken. I've had time to prepare for this, but I don't think Jack has ever seen the end coming.

Softer, I repeat, "I wasn't taking advantage of you. You bought my screenplay before we were ever going out, remember? I wouldn't hurt you like that. I love you."

His eyes glaze with tears as he studies my face. "Then, why this? Why now?"

Before I can find a gentle way to couch it, the truth forces its flat, emotionless self from my throat. "Because just now, when we were fighting? I thought of how great a scene this would be."

He doesn't respond.

I go on. "I am always writing, Jack. It's a part of my brain that I can't shut off. And it's a part of me I'm proud of, even though it makes me do stupid, selfish things. Maybe I'll never be able to be with anyone. Maybe I'll end up married to my work, or however you want to put it. But the worst thing for me would be to take that part of myself and put it out there so the whole world can call me a fraud."

I want him to understand it, so it won't hurt as much. And so it will make me feel less guilty. God, what a terrible person I am.

He laughs softly and looks down at his hands. "Yeah, all right. But just a couple things."

"Yeah?"

"The whole world isn't talking about you. They don't know who you are."

I don't have a super-sized Hollywood ego, but it's still a direct hit. Not because I want to be world famous, but because he said it deliberately to hurt me. The thought of Jack wanting to hurt me is too big and horrible to fit inside my chest, and I feel like I'm two seconds from exploding in anger or tears. I don't know which.

"And I was…" He stops, swallows, and tries again, but his voice is still raw. "I was the guy who was going to stick by you all the way. But you go ahead. Marry your work. I'm sure you'll be very happy together."

He gets out of the car without another word. I want to call him back, to tell him I've changed my mind, but I haven't. And it's too late, anyway. Nothing I can say will undo all the things I've just told him, or make him forget that this will probably always be lurking in the back of my mind.

It's done. There's no looking back. I watch him walk to the house, head down, hands in his pockets. The rain sticks his shirt to his skin.

I want him. I want my career and my name and something of my own, on my terms. I can't have all of that at once. I have to give him up.

## Chapter Seven

I twist the straw paper in my hands as I stare out the window, waiting for Jack. I'm at our secret sushi place, and he's running late.

*Not* our *sushi place*, I remind myself. *The one that we usually come to. For business reasons.*

This isn't the first time one of us has dated post-break up. It isn't even the first time one of us dated during our friends-with-kinky-benefits relationship. I don't have any romantic designs on Jack, anymore, and our D/s arrangement has been on hold more than once as I figured things out with a romantic prospect.

But I don't want to go on hold, again. I don't want Jack to have any prospects. It's maddeningly selfish of me, and I wish I could make that irrational emotional response take a hike. I'm just threatened by Madison Avery because she's so damn young and smooth and pert. It's difficult to live in L.A. and not do a little body coveting. Plus, Jack doesn't date, so the fact that he might be just freaks me out.

The reason I *should* be freaking out this morning is that stupid fanfic. It's been blasting across Twitter and Tumblr and Facebook and god alone knew where else people complain about shit online. I would have rather slept off my flight all day, but Jack wanted to see me, *now*. Probably because if he didn't, we would both be too distracted to have a good scene tomorrow night.

"Sorry I'm late," he says as he breezes through the door. The waitress, not exactly overwhelmed with tables right at opening, hurries over and takes his drink order. She tries to give him a menu, but like me, he politely declines. "I'll have the spicy tuna roll, edamame, and one unagi sashimi, please."

"Red Dragon, please." I wait until she leaves to say anything, but Jack beats me to it.

"So, what the hell happened in Atlanta?"

I shrug. I can tell him every inane detail of my travel and dance around recounting what was easily in the top five most awkward moments I've ever personally witnessed, but what would be the point? We both know what we're here about. "It was so painfully embarrassing."

"For you, or her?" Jack takes off his jacket and hangs it across the back of his chair like it's a cheap cardigan.

"Put it this way: if she didn't feel it, I certainly felt it for her. But my hands are clean."

"Oh, so that's your only concern, huh?" Jack says with a lop-sided smile.

"Obviously," I scoff. "Seriously, though. What's going on with this?"

"Legal's keeping an eye on it." He shrugs and rolls his eyes. "I mean, what are we going to do about it? The script is done, the casting is underway—"

I hate that my mind popped directly to Madison Avery and not the heart of the matter. "So, nothing. They're just going to go forward with a stolen property."

"Allegedly stolen." He's cautious with his words. "MollyCuddles94 hasn't made a move, yet."

Jack's first concern is the studio and, by extension, his job. And that's fine. But...

"What do *you* think?" I ask, hoping he's a decent enough person to give me the right answer.

"She stole it," he answers automatically.

"You read it?"

He scoffs. "No, I'm not in the habit of reading fanfic of my own movies. I read a summary on a blog. Did you read it?"

I nod and sip my water.

"What did you think?"

"I think I'm going to hide my notebooks from her." I laugh. "Not that she would want to steal from me, since I'm such a hack."

"Did she say that to you?" His eyes widen.

"No. There would have been blood on the walls." But it makes me wonder if she said that to him. "What happens if MollyCuddles94 does pop out of the woodwork?"

"Nothing, at first. Before anything would even make it to court, we're going to be filming."

"So, we're just going to ahead with this? Even though we know she ripped someone else off?" That doesn't sit right with me. "Darkness Standing" isn't a literary masterpiece, but if it's someone else's, how can I justify stealing it, again?

"My assumption is that the studio would settle and pay MollyCuddles94 whatever he or she is owed. Or a percentage on royalties or box office. Something like that. And it would probably come out of Lynn's pocket. We didn't know it was plagiarized when we bought it."

"So, Macrocosm didn't know about this potential controversy that apparently has been whispered all over the internet for the past three years?" I find that difficult to believe. For a property this big, they would have had their interns googling it every day.

Jack doesn't say anything.

"Oh my god."

He holds up his hands. "I was one person out of a whole team—"

"Wow." I'm so disgusted I can barely look at him.

"I didn't know anything beyond that there were rumors floating around about that book. That's all. Lynn signed an affidavit stating that the book was her original work. I wouldn't have gotten you involved if I thought there would be any legal repercussions."

"I'm not upset about the legal. I'm upset about the moral implication here. I'm complicit in helping steal another writer's work."

"And, if they pursue this, then you'll be complicit in making MollyCuddles94 a lot of money."

This was something Jack never understood about how his craft differed from mine. When he worked, he became someone else. They went up on the screen, not him. But, when a writer writes, they put themselves on the screen. I can't play the role of a person whose actions don't concern me.

He leans in and lowers his voice, that irritating I'm-so-rational-right-now thing he does that I can't stand. "Look, I know this bothers you. I'm not trying to be dismissive. But the wheels are already in motion. I don't have anything to tell you that will make you feel better. And I don't like the idea of helping advance Lynn's career, believe me. Not anymore. But we can't be the people who hurt the movie by walking away over this. MollyCuddles94 is the only person who has any legal standing to go after Lynn."

He's infuriatingly right. I can walk away from the project and get myself blacklisted at the studios—and probably hurt Jack's career, too—and it won't help anyone at all. It won't put money in MollyCuddles94's pockets. It won't make Lynn unpopular with her legion of diehard fans. Jack is right. All we can do is move forward.

He sits back as the waitress places his tea on the table and waits until she leaves to ask me, "Are you available tonight?"

"Available how?" I ask cautiously. "It's not Tuesday."

"Oh, I know when Tuesday is." He smirks over the rim of his cup. "No, I have script notes from Lynn."

The noise that comes out of me is shocking and inhuman.

Jack snorts his tea and sputters as he chokes on it. I scrabble to hand him a napkin.

"Sorry," I say, but I'm kind of not sorry. I wish I would have let loose with a primal scream, because that would have more accurately captured the way I feel about god damn Lynn and her fuck-ass stupid notes.

"There are a few changes she wanted me to make," he says, wiping tea off of his fingers. "And I'm not a writer."

"Yeah, I am. And on this movie, even. So, why does she want you to make changes?"

"She doesn't trust your judgement." Jack shakes his head. "They're mostly about word choices. There are some lines she feels are too stilted, or missing, or not 'capturing the authenticity of the novel'. The usual Lynn stuff."

"Well, send them to me." I don't want to spend my night working on stolen property. "I don't need supervision."

"That remains to be seen." He winks at me, and my heart tickles. Even with years between then and now, there are still moments when he makes me feel...

"I know you can do it on your own," he goes on. "But I'd like to help. I'll sound more convincing when I tell her I made all of these changes by myself."

"Maybe she'll hang it up on the refrigerator." I laugh at my own joke. "What time were you thinking?"

"Eight?"

Okay, so he's not scheduling early enough to make it to a date afterward. "Okay. You know where to find me."

"I always do." His eyes lock on mine, and he stares at me a little longer than seems normal.

The moment is broken by the arrival of our food, and I wonder if I imagined it all.

\*\*\*\*

"You're calling me to analyze a look he gave you?"

Distance cannot cushion the blunt force of Sherri's tough-love tone.

"I know, this is way too *Sex and The City*." I push one hand through my sleek, straightened hair. Which I straightened just because I wanted to check and make sure my straightener still worked. It has nothing to do with the fact that Jack will be over in twenty minutes.

"It's way too middle school," Sherri corrects me. "What happened to 'we're just good friends who do freaky shit together'?"

"Nothing happened to it. I mean, other than he started seeing someone."

"And, now, you want what you can't have?"

"Exactly." It would be so easy to chalk it up to such simple jealousy, but that wasn't it, either. "No. I mean, I don't want him. I think I feel like I'm supposed to want him."

"Uh huh."

"Seriously, though. It was my choice to end our relationship, so I could build my career. But it's built, now, and I don't really see an obstacle to the two of us, you know?" I squinch up my face, dreading her response.

"I can think of an obstacle," Sherri says dryly. "He thinks he made you. Do you really think that attitude has gone away?"

Ugh, she's so right, and I hate it. "It's been a long time, though. He's definitely matured—"

"Enough to date twenty-year-olds. Yeah, super mature."

I swear I can *hear* her eyes roll.

"Do whatever you want," she continues. "But keep in mind that if you try a second time and it doesn't work out, you can basically kiss your friendship and your working relationship goodbye. Guys with egos like Jack's don't stand up to repeated battering."

"You say that like I'm going to hit him," I say.

She points out, "You do hit him. Every Tuesday night."

My skin gets hot. That's another complication, one I guess I haven't thought too deeply about. What happens to our weekly session if we open another can of romantic worms? Is it worth risking our friendship *and* our relationship as Dom and sub?

*Is it worth the risk to not confess your feelings and just never know what could have been?*

I don't even know what my feelings are, yet.

My doorbell buzzes. I glance up at the clock. "Are you freaking kidding me?"

"He's early." Sherri sounds defeated. She has this whole theory on what it means when guys show up early or late or on time.

"Well, don't sound too enthusiastic. It might not mean anything other than he left work on time." But a part of me hopes that's not it. I want him to be eager to see me. I need that reassurance.

*You didn't need it before he was interested in someone else*, I remind myself as I hang up with Sherri.

Because it's not Tuesday, Jack doesn't use his key. He waits for me to come to the door. When I open it, I find him not fresh from the office, but dressed for his off hours; a slate t-shirt that I know without touching will be butter-soft, once-dark jeans with visible wear at the knees, and Birkenstocks. Birkenstocks, for Christ's sake.

"I brought beer," he says, holding up a six pack and trying to keep his laptop bag from hitting the door frame.

"Come in." I take the beer to the kitchen and pop four of them into the fridge. Then, I take the tops off the last two and carry them into the living room, where he's already taking out his computer. Mine is open on the couch, and I hope nothing embarrassing is on the screen.

"I want to get this sewn up tonight," he explains, frowning at his laptop. "I am officially sick of Kathy Muller's voice."

"I always expect her to refer to Lynn as 'The Presence'. I'm surprised she doesn't curtsey before she leaves the room."

"I don't know, I think some of the shine of being Lynn Baldwin's assistant is wearing off," he says, but before I can question him, he looks up and adds, "Brace for impact. We cast Damian."

"It's not who she wanted?" I should *not* feel a thrill of glee at that, because Lynn's wrath greatly inconveniences the production. But casting isn't a part of the production I have to worry about, so I don't have to brace myself for anything.

"Wren Taylor."

Now, that *is* a surprise. "I thought he wasn't even on the shortlist."

"He wasn't. But his agent lobbied to get him an audition, and he was very good. Almost supernaturally good. That show isn't doing him any favors."

The show Jack refers to is an over-the-top cable drama about a detective who specializes in reading facial cues. It's Taylor's breakout role, and it's made him a fan favorite. But I'm surprised that he got to read for Damian.

"He really connects with Damian Bennett, I guess," Jack adds with a shrug.

"I pity whoever he's dating." I don't want to talk about casting with Jack. I don't want either of us to bring up Madison Avery. "Okay, let's take a look at what she thinks needs your special touch."

"Well, for starters, she wants that aftercare scene you added cut. She won't move on that," he says with an apologetic wince.

I think he's expecting a fight. He's not going to get one from me tonight. "That's fine. She's the one who wrote the book. I can't get blamed for it."

"Yikes. Okay. Cut, then," he murmurs to himself. "So, next up, she hates that you've moved the second date scene to a private dining room and out of the main restaurant."

"That's stupid," I say without hesitation. "Private dining room is going to be cheaper and easier to film."

"I agree, and that's what I told her." He taps away at his keyboard. He doesn't type, so much as hunts-and-pecks. "I think Marion will tell her the same thing."

So far, these changes sound pretty simple. "So, you agree. We're keeping it in a private room."

"Absolutely." He nods, and I wonder why he didn't just sign off on this one before coming over. He scans his screen and says, "Okay. Don't freak out over this one."

"I'm going to freak out," I warn him.

"The very last line."

My back teeth clench. Lynn has already informed me that she feels the last line of Ella's dialogue—"Always"—should be included, and no argument to the contrary will sway her. "It's immediately going to take people out of *Beautiful Darkness* and directly into Harry Potter. Marion isn't going to give in on this one."

"No, she isn't. And things are getting testy." He pinches the bridge of his nose. "I was thinking maybe you could come up with something that has the same emotional punch?"

"You want me to come up with a synonym for always? Because you don't have a thesaurus at your house?" I shake my head. "What's going on? Why are you really here?"

He makes a frustrated noise. "I'm really here because I really need help with this. I'm not a writer, Jessica. This doesn't come as easily to me as it does to you."

"Forever," I reply. Now, I'm the one getting testy. "Why not 'forever'? It will still fit on a Hot Topic t-shirt."

I can see it, now. Cheap black cotton v-neck, swirly silver lettering. "Forever..." Even my imagination is bitchy.

"What other motive do you think I had for coming here tonight?" he asks, jerking me back to the present. Testy appears to be catching.

*I thought you might be coming over to try to rekindle a relationship with me because I saw you went to a movie premiere with a woman almost half my age, and I'm intimidated.* I can't say that. And I can't think up a convincing lie. "I thought you might have been coming over here because of Madison Avery."

I wait for his denial. The weird scrunched-up face he does. The slight backwards lean of his neck, like he's physically shying away from how ridiculous I'm being.

It doesn't come.

Instead, he rubs one hand over his face and lets out a long exhale. "Yeah. So, about that."

"I saw it on the Entertainment Channel," I say, my voice barely a whisper. I clear my throat. "Is this where we have our big conversation?"

He shakes his head. "No. Nothing like that. We're not—"

The "we" bothers me more than it should.

"It's not an exclusive thing," he says finally. "We've been seeing each other, but I've made it clear that we're not dating."

"Are you sleeping together?" I don't really want to know, but I have to. Not for purely emotional reasons, but because I'm his Dom. We might not fuck, but I deserve to know if the partner I'm playing with is being responsible with other people.

He tucks his chin to his chest and coughs a little. "Just a couple of times."

I don't answer him, because I can't trust my own voice. All I can think about is Madison Avery's toned, tan body writhing all over him. It's easy to imagine it looking like a scene from a movie, since they're both movie stars. *She gets pimples on her ass just like everyone else*, I tell myself, borrowing Sherri's go-to confidence builder.

"So, were you actually going to tell me any of this before our session tomorrow?" I ask finally. "Or is that cancelled?"

"No, not cancelled. Not unless you want to," he says, a hopeful note in his voice. "This isn't serious. Not yet."

*Not yet.* I wonder when "yet" will be.

"I know how this looks," he goes on, almost guiltily. "And I know how you must be feeling, right now."

My face burns with a sudden rush of embarrassment. Have I been obvious? Shameless?

"And I promise," he continues, like he's on trial, "I'm not going to do anything to hurt her career."

*Okay...*

"That's good to hear. I guess?" I say, pulling my legs up to fold them beneath me. I need to be physically compact, so I don't feel as vulnerable. "Why would you think that was my concern?"

"Because of how we broke up." He shrugs. "The whole thing over your career. I don't want people to think she got cast as Ella because of my influence."

"Didn't she?" That sounds bitter and accusatory. I quickly add, "Because you were talking to her at that party before casting even started."

"No, I swear. I had no idea she was even being considered."

I believe him, because he has no reason to lie to me about it. However, the press is going to think he's lying when he says it to them, and they're going to definitely think Madison Avery is lying when she recites that line.

A choice lies ahead of me, a choice between begrudging good and gratifying evil. Because I know Jack's dating history. I know how afraid he is to be used for his name and power. And it would be so easy to use my position as his friend to sow seeds of doubt in his mind. The material is already there; Madison Avery is built from all the same parts as the women who *would* date Jack to get into a movie, and he's probably already given a lot of thought to the possibility. But a good friend wouldn't prey on that insecurity to get what she wants. That would make me almost as bad.

Wouldn't it?

I settle on, "Well, it's not me you have to convince. I know you. I believe you. But will anyone else?"

"Yeah, I've thought about that." He pauses. "All of that aside, I'm not ready to stop subbing for you, if you're not ready for me to."

"It's not about being ready. It's about being honest." My throat tightens. "And you were honest. But don't blindside me, when the time comes."

"If the time comes. Madison is a really cool girl, but…"

"But she's a girl." It's not an insult. It's just a fact.

He nods.

"You're not looking for my opinion, but I'm going to give it to you." And I can do it without it being in my own interests alone, because it's something he needs to hear. "You've never wanted people to think you're cliché Hollywood guy. And you know what they're going to think about this."

"They're going to think I'm cliché Hollywood guy." He runs a hand through his hair and looks over at me from under his arm. "I'm a mess, aren't I?"

"You always have been. Might as well stick with what works."

He leans back and unrolls his arm casually across the back of the couch, behind me. "I hate this movie."

"You won't be the only one. I promise." The urge to relax against the cushions and let his arm drape around me is strong. Too strong for my weak constitution. I give in. My hair brushes his arm. That's how aware of him I am. I can feel him with my hair.

Sherri is right. I'm in a dangerous place.

"So, I did have an ulterior motive for coming here tonight," he says with a bashful shrug. "I just didn't realize it."

He holds my gaze for an unfairly long amount of time. Unfair because he can't know what I'm thinking. He can't assure me of anything, because even I don't know what assurances I need.

I have to look away. "So, what's next on the list?"

I lean forward to peek at his laptop screen. I never get a chance. Jack swoops in and his mouth is on mine. How long has it been since we've kissed? It doesn't matter because he kisses me like he's been waiting a century, but it feels like no time has passed at all.

I should pull back, but I don't want to be the first to end it. He might think I'm not interested. Am I interested? But, if he pulls away first, what will that mean for me?

I don't have the ability to think too deeply on it. Jack's mouth demands all of my attention. He's good. God, he's good. And I've needed this so, so badly.

Why did I ever give him up? Why did this ever feel wrong to me?

He pulls back first, and it doesn't feel as crushing as it could. We need space. I need perspective. He definitely does, because not five minutes ago, we were talking about the girl he's been fucking.

"I'm sorry," he says immediately. "That wasn't—"

"Don't worry about it," I say, like he accidentally stepped on my foot rather than kissed me without permission and knocked us off the emotional tightrope we've been walking for half a decade.

"I think I need time to clear my head. I think—" He stops himself. "I don't know what I think."

My heart twists in my chest. "I think we need to cancel tomorrow night. While you figure things out. Just for the week, to give you some breathing room."

He grimaces, but nods. "You're right. Probably not a great idea to show up with confused emotions."

My breath turns to cement in my lungs. Confused emotions? What the hell does he mean by that? My emotions were already confused, and now, they're downright baffled.

"Over Madison, I mean," he adds quickly, and my heart plummets.

I hope the thickness in my throat isn't audible as I swallow. "Yes. Let's be smart about this. The last thing I want is for you to sub drop because you've got all this on your mind."

His smile is small and relieved and uncertain. "There you go, again. Looking out for both of us."

March 27, 2011

I forgot that Jack still has a key, until he knocks on my door. He's come through the gate, but stopped short of barging in entirely. Still, that gate feels important to me. It's like he's breached the first line of my defenses.

I open the door just enough to see him standing outside with a container of soup.

"Hey," I greet him, pulling my heavy cotton quilt tighter around my shoulders. "I'm actually not feeling so good, right now, so—"

"I know," he says as my gaze moves from his face to the soup. "I shouldn't have come."

I want to snap back, *then why did you?* but I can't say anything, so I just stand there staring at him, hoping snot isn't dripping from my nose.

"Look. I know I shouldn't have said a lot of the things I said. You were just being honest, and in a way, you were looking out for both of us. You didn't trap us in an unhealthy relationship." He looks down, scuffing the toes of his sneakers on my raffia door mat. "Anyway, I heard you were sick. And I wanted to help."

He hands the container to me.

"Wow. Uh." This is too much for someone with a 101-degree fever to process. I don't want him to think I'm giving him the brush off, though I would be perfectly justified in doing so. You don't just show up at your ex's house without warning. But this is *Jack*. So, I push the door open. "Come in."

He steps inside cautiously. I understand what he's feeling. This is the first time we've seen each other since we broke up a month ago, and now, he looks out of place in my apartment. In my life. I've erased him without intending to.

For my survival, I guess. Because nothing has hurt as much as realizing that Jack and I aren't ever going to work.

"How did you hear I was sick?" I ran through the list of possible traitors in my mind. I isolated myself like I had a disease in the wake of our breakup. I hadn't talked to some of my friends in weeks.

"Dani," he explains with a wave. "You posted it on Facebook."

Right. Facebook. That fucking thing.

"I'm sorry, Jess." He puts his hands in his pockets because he doesn't know what to do with them. He never does. "I said some—"

"Don't. I'm too stuffed up." I indicate my general sinus area. "Whatever you're going to say, we can say it when I'm not so congested."

"Right." He scratches his forehead with the back of his thumb. "Have you been to the doctor?"

He knows I don't have insurance. I shake my head.

"Do you want to go? My treat?"

My cold isn't serious enough to warrant a doctor visit. At least, not yet. Still, I should thank him. Instead, what comes out is, "Why are you doing this?"

"You're sick. Soup and doctors make sick people feel better."

"Not the soup." I hate that I have to pause to blow my nose. "Why are you here, checking up on me after—"

"After you dumped me?" He says it like he's popping a balloon. The words are harsh and shocking, and they end the suspense between us.

"I would have said 'broken up', but..."

"Then, you would have just been making yourself feel better. You dumped me. Blindsided me, actually." He laughs, short, dismayed. "But you're my best friend. And, when you dumped me, I lost my girlfriend *and* my best friend on the same day. That's cliché and stupid, but I don't want it to be that way. If you don't want to be my girlfriend, fine. I'm a big boy. I can take it. But please, don't stop being my friend.

Don't stop being the girl who gave me life advice during a lap dance."

In spite of my hurting heart and aching head, a laugh burbles out of me. Like, literally. The noise of the trapped phlegm in my chest startles us both. The laugh quickly turns into an epic coughing fit, and his expression grows alarmed.

"Okay, best friend or most bitter enemy, I can't listen to someone drown." He pulls his Blackberry from his pocket and punches buttons before I can protest. "Rick, this is J-Dog—"

"J-Dog?" I gasp between hacks.

He gives me a thumbs-down and turns away. "Texting you an address. Got a friend who needs a cocktail."

"Ugh." I groan and shuffle into the living room. Jack's stupid cocktail. Well, not Jack's. Jack's doctor's cocktail. That progression of words made it sound even shadier to my ears. Lots of L.A. doctors make house calls, but the idea of someone jabbing vitamin injections into my ass right in my living room seems weird to me.

Jack finishes his call and joins me, dropping onto the couch beside me. "Probably won't be more than an hour. Do you want your soup?"

I give in and nod gratefully. When he returns, I wait until he puts the soup and spoon on the coffee table before I say, "I'm not your most bitter enemy."

He frowns questioningly.

"You said 'best friend or most bitter enemy.' I'm not your most bitter enemy." I draw my feet up to tuck them beneath me.

"Maybe it's too early to joke about that kind of stuff." He shrugs and lifts the lid of the container. "I don't think of you as my enemy."

"Not anymore?" I tease him, but then immediately collapse into choking on mucus, again.

"Not at all. The shittiest part of us breaking up was knowing that you were right, and not being able to do anything to change the situation."

His linguistic concession isn't lost on me. I pick up the soup carefully and slurp the broth straight from the container.

"That's sexy," he says, chuckling.

I hold up my middle finger and swallow. "I don't think you actually wanted to help me get over being sick at all. You just wanted to make sure that the next time we saw each other, you looked better than me."

"You caught me." He leans over and kisses my forehead.

We both freeze. There's no doubt in my mind that habit had forced his action, but it's uncomfortable and too familiar for two people trying to distance themselves from their romantic connection.

He leans back slowly, like he's trying to not startle a cobra. "Sorry."

"No, it's okay. I know what that was about." I try to laugh it off, but knowing why something happened and being okay with the thing that happened are vastly different things. "Maybe we retreat to 'acquaintance distance' with the physicality, okay? Just until we figure this all out."

"Like, until I stop being in love with you?" His expression hardens, then crumples to a kindness that's far more heartbreaking. "I mean, that's going to happen, right? I will eventually move on and fall out of love with you."

"Of course it will." What a weird thing to assure someone. "And someday, I'll fall out of love with you. And we'll fall in love with other people. And then, we won't care as much about soup and awkward forehead kisses."

He shakes his head. "No. I might fall out of love with you. But I'll never stop caring about you."

## Chapter Eight

After weeks of writing and rewriting while listening to only the character voices in my head, a table read is usually a relief.

Usually.

Today, the idea of listening to my much-contested work being read aloud in front of Lynn Baldwin is about as look-forward-to-able as swallowing handfuls of aquarium rocks.

The main cast—thankfully settled now after weeks of media speculation and in-house waffling—the executive producers, Jack, Marion, and I are all crammed around a table in a Macrocosm conference room. Lynn is here, too, sitting between Marion and me. A few production assistants are on hand to replenish water bottles when necessary and to film the read-through for later reference. And of course, Kathy Muller is there, huddled in a corner with her planners and devices. Lynn has brought her husband along, as well. He's scowling, though I think he's just trying to give off an air of serious business.

I check and double check my pens and highlighters like a gladiator about to enter an arena would prepare his weapons. Across the table, Madison Avery, her hair pulled up in a sloppy bun that only gorgeous twenty-somethings can pull off without looking haggard, studies the script on the table in front of her. The pages are curled at the edges, and post-its stick out from the sides like flags. She's read the script more than once, and she's come prepared. I can't help but admire that dedication; her love interest hasn't done nearly that much. Wren Taylor's script doesn't look like it's ever been opened. He slouches in his chair in a gray hoodie and too-long denim shorts, constantly fidgeting and readjusting his backwards ball cap.

I glance to Marion. Her eyes narrow as she watches him. She's already taking notes, even if she's not writing them down, yet.

"You wanna kick this off?" Jack asks. He's seated to Marion's left, safely out of my line of sight. I absolutely can't be distracted by his presence today, if I'm going to do my job effectively.

We've barely spoken since that kiss. It's been two Tuesdays. Not a single call.

*Focus up,* I order myself as Marion stands.

"Good morning, everybody. You all know me already, I'm Marion Cross. I'll be directing *Beautiful Darkness.* This is Jack Martin, our producer—"

My gaze snaps to Madison. Her expression is impassive.

"—and this is Jessica Yates, who wrote the lovely script we'll be reading today." Marion puts a slight lean on the word "lovely". She's either reassuring me or warning Lynn. "And that's Lynn Baldwin, author of *Beautiful Darkness.* "

Kathy Muller gives a little "whoo!" from her corner, and everyone around the table chuckles.

I've always loved the atmosphere in a read-through. It's the first time that the movie feels real. Sitting in my apartment tapping away at my keyboard or attending pre-production meetings is a lot of talk and spaced out action. It's planning for a vacation that feels like it will never come. The table read is the moment you finally get behind the wheel and take to the open road.

The cast goes around the table, introducing themselves. For some of them, it's the first time they're meeting. It's the first time the main cast has been assembled in one place.

"What we're going to do today is a read through." Marion emphasizes the space in "read through". "Don't worry too much about acting it out. Give me what you can, but don't stress. I'm going to be listening to the script more than your performances."

Oh, that doesn't put me on the spot at all.

"May I say something?" Lynn asks, half-raising her hand.
Marion's eyebrows rise. "Sure."

Lynn addresses the cast directly. "I just want to thank you all for being so perfect. Even though you're blond, Madison."

Madison laughs. Jack does, too. It's a joke just between the three of them.

"Okay, let's get started." Marion nods to a young PA sitting at the end of the table.

He clears his throat. "Fade In: Los Angeles skyline. Day. Interior Ella's bedroom. We see Ella Vaughn, a pale young brunette woman, standing in front of her mirror. She's twenty-two and has just been hired for her first post-college job as a reporter for the L.A. Herald. She is determined and focused as she ties her hair back in a red ribbon. Her roommate, Caroline Devereux, leans into the reflection. Caroline is tall, model-pretty, and blond; everything that Ella is not."

Kara Gifford, who's been cast as Ella's roommate, delivers the first line of dialogue in a clear, confident voice. "You're not really wearing that, are you?"

"What's wrong with this?" Madison answers as Ella.

"You don't look like someone who would blend in at an underground fighting ring," Kara/Caroline responds.

"I don't have to blend in. I just have to look like a reporter—"

"Hold!"

Madison stutters to a stop, mid-line. Marion leans forward to look at Lynn, who has her hand politely half-raised again.

Lynn claps her hands together softly, her bracelets clacking. "One thing. Ella is still using contractions? I thought we discussed this."

"Let's hold our notes until the end," Marion suggests, a polite dismissal, but a dismissal nonetheless. This is Marion's territory, now. She isn't going to let Lynn call the shots the way Jack did, regardless of how much creative control she's been promised.

But, like a raptor in *Jurassic Park*, Lynn has to test the fence. "I don't see the harm in just trying."

Marion opens her mouth to protest, but I speak over her because what the hell? The mood has gone from "fun ride through a dinosaur amusement park" to "is that T-Rex escaping?" in a single tense interruption. The mood in the room is ruined already.

"We could try just the rest of the scene that way." I shrug innocently and nod toward Madison. She's a good actress, so when she can't pull off the clunky dialogue, it's going to be obvious that it's not working.

Marion turns her head just slightly to look at me from the corner of her eye, as if to say, *clever girl*.

"Do you think you can do that, Madison?" Marion asks.

"Um…" Madison flips a couple of pages. "Sure. Can you give me just a second?"

"Absolutely. We'll start over, when you're ready."

Madison picks up a pen and leans over her script to mark up her dialogue. After a few long, silent moments, she lifts her head. "Okay. Just this scene, right?"

"Just this scene," Marion promises, because everyone sitting at the table knows that this change isn't going to be permanent.

Everyone except Lynn, who leans forward, eager to hear her exact words spoken aloud.

"Fade in," the PA repeats, a little louder on those words than the ones that follow. Kara delivers her line, "You're not really wearing that, are you?" and Madison follows with, "What is wrong with this?"

"You don't look like someone who would blend in at an underground fighting ring."

"I do not have to blend in. I just have to look like a reporter. Because that is what I am."

The PA shifts in his chair. "Interior, Ella and Caroline's living room, day. Ella puts her coat on as Caroline makes herself comfortable on the couch. It's clear that Caroline won't be doing much today."

"Just be careful, all right? I'm not going to be able to relax knowing that you're hanging out with a bunch of degenerates," Kara reads.

"I would hate to cut into your precious daytime television schedule. I know you are looking forward to finding out who the father is." Madison sounds like a robot. It's exactly how I expected her to sound.

I chance a look at Lynn. She's captivated.

"If you see anyone cute, bring him home," Kara says, her spunky delivery earning a few quiet laughs.

"I will not see anyone cute," Madison replies. "They are probably all going to be missing teeth and covered with tattoos."

"Cut to interior Damian Bennet's closet, day," the PA reads. "We see only flashes of Damian Bennet. His bare chest. His hands as they fasten his shirt cuffs. He is a man in total control at all times, and it shows in both his movements and the stringent organization of his environment. Cut to interior Damian Bennet's office, day. We walk behind Damian, never seeing his face as he strides confidently through the halls. Office staff scurry back and forth as he approaches, everyone desperate to look busy. Cut to interior Bennet Corp. lobby, day. Ella approaches the security desk. Her conservative casual clothing and her red hair bow make her stand out in the starkly neutral surrounding. Out of her element, Ella approaches the security desk.

"Hi, I'm here to see Damian Bennet?"

Beside me, Lynn "tsk"s and scribbles something on a post-it. Over "I'm?" I realize my jaw is painfully clenched, and I reach up to surreptitiously rub it as I listen to the scene—which we absolutely could not cut—of Ella being briefed on the do's and don'ts of meeting Damian Bennet. Because the part of Damian's assistant hasn't been cast, yet, the PA reads those lines, as well. But the part everyone is waiting for is the moment that Ella and Damian meet. When it arrives, the creaks of chairs and some whispers of fabric ripple around the table as people subtly adjust in their seats.

"Interior, Damian's office, day. Damian sits in an office chair facing the window. As Ella nervously approaches the desk, he slowly turns."

"Ella Vaughn?" Wren reads.

"Y-yes. That's me. I'm here from the L.A. Herald? Jackson—"

"—Fosco sent you. I know." Wren is surprisingly in-character for a guy who's slouched over a script, absent-mindedly rubbing the back of his neck. "You're here for the story on the Malaysian farmers we recently bailed out."

"No. I'm here for the story about the Serpent Ring." Madison reads Ella's line with a little more confidence.

"Fosco shouldn't have told you about that." Wren says, his voice icy and calm. He's exactly what I've imagined Damian Bennet to be. "It makes you a liability."

He growls through his dialogue. He's read the book.

"Let me guess. Now, you have to kill me?" Madison's delivery garners a laugh from the room.

But not from Lynn.

Because that line isn't from the book. I added it into the latest revisions, which she apparently hasn't bothered to read. Jack leans back in his chair and spares me the briefest, angriest glance.

Fuck him. It's a good line.

In the book, Damian's dialogue wasn't interrupted by Ella's. His lines resume seamlessly. "You can't handle the Serpent Ring."

"I'm tougher than I look," Madison reads, to another laugh. She looks up, and her gaze snaps to Jack, her smile small and secret.

I don't care. My stupid romantic or not-romantic feelings can't ruin the elation I feel at hearing those laughs, seeing the reactions. For the first time since I finished the rough draft, I feel like this movie might actually work.

Like that, the atmosphere is back.

\*\*\*\*

It doesn't last. After the read through is over and we've thanked everyone, Jack, Marion, Lynn—with husband and assistant in tow— –and I go to Jack's office. We all walk together in a crowded mass that blocks the halls, but we don't talk. We have never been so strained, and we've never worked so hard and so unconvincingly to pretend not to notice.

Once we're inside and mostly all seated, Jack shuts his door. "Okay. I think that went really well. Let's do some notes."

"Can we talk about that chemistry?" Marion asks, more enthusiastic than I've ever seen her about this project. "Madison and Wren were fantastic."

Lynn's husband whispers something to her, then addresses the room with a sharp, "No."

Our heads collectively swivel, and I gape at him.

"The chemistry was fine," he amends. "The chemistry is not the issue. The writing—"

"Every word of dialogue came straight from your book, Lynn," Marion begins coolly, ignoring "Mr. Inspiration" entirely. "So, let's not get back into that, again."

"Not every word," Jack says calmly.

My blood rushes straight to my ears, and my throat constricts in anger. I can't believe it. I can't believe he's sold me out like this. And right in front of me, as though I'm not even in the room. All of his talk about being on my side and—

"I added some things to it," Jack says. "When you asked for revisions. Again. And you were given a chance to review those changes, which were necessary for the film."

"Oh, really?" Lynn practically puffs up like an exotic bird. "Joking about Damian stalking Ella? Making a crack about him killing her? Ella would never joke about that."

"A film is not a book, Lynn!" Jack finally snaps. "We had to make artistic decisions that would make the damn thing watchable."

"Are you yelling at my wife?" Mr. Inspiration demands, going red to the tips of his ears and the top of his shiny bald head.

"No. I'm putting my foot down, like everyone should have from the start!"

Lynn bolts to her feet. Kathy shrinks back in her chair.

"I am leaving!" It's an announcement and a threat, with Lynn giving Jack the option to change his mind and beg her forgiveness.

He doesn't. He stands and gestures a path to the door. "When you're ready to actually collaborate on this movie, you know my number."

Lynn stares at him in disbelief. He doesn't flinch. Their silent power struggle feels like an eternity, but it only lasts as long as Lynn can go without blinking. Then, she picks up her purse, thrusts it at Kathy, and strides out, entourage in her wake.

Mr. Inspiration is thorough enough to slam the door.

The three of us sit in stunned silence, until Marion says, "Jack."

"I know." He runs a hand through his hair. "I know."

It's a good thing one of us does. I glance over and see the script Lynn has left behind, sitting on the glass topped coffee table.

"What are you doing?" Marion asks as I lean to pick the pages up.

"Might as well look at her notes." I flip through the pages, watching the pen marks and crossed-out lines add up.

"Jesus."

I didn't realize Jack has come to stand behind me, and he watches over my shoulder as I turn the pages.

"Does she like anything we've done?" Marion asks, leaning in closer. Soon, we're all reading Lynn's preposterous notes aloud, cackling with mixed dismay and glee.

"She is fucking married to not using contractions." Jack groans.

"Even Madison couldn't pull that off without sounding like a robot," Marion says and, to me, adds, "Nice strategy, by the way."

"Jess can be downright devious when she puts her mind to it." Jack squeezes my shoulder in encouragement.

"Well, Lynn's not going to win that battle. Critics will rip it to shreds. Even more so than they will already."

Jack frowns. "Do you think so?"

"I think people have been rooting for Lynn Baldwin to fail since the book came out," I answer in Marion's place. "Thanks for taking the fall over that murder line."

"This is a good movie, Jess." Jack sits in the chair to my right. "You made it a good movie. And we're going to make a good movie. The one you wrote."

My chest swells with pride and hope and pleasure at being praised by my superior. Even if that superior is Jack. Because I'm pathetic and constantly seeking approval.

"I'll make the apology call," Marion volunteers. She takes the script from me. "And look this over. If I can promise a few compromises, she'll think I'm on her side."

"Oh, so you're good cop?" I joke.

"Which makes me bad cop," Jack says without any humor.

"Then, what does that make me?" I ask with a grim laugh. "The victim?"

Jack doesn't answer. "Flattery will only get us so far with Lynn. We're going to have to come up with some way of forcing her to work with us."

"Get an exec in the room? So, she has to be on her best behavior?" Marion suggests. "It's worked before."

"But are they going to actually throw their weight around with this one?" I hate to admit it, but Lynn really does have the upper hand. "She just sold a sequel. This is a franchise, now. They're going to want to keep her happy."

Jack scrubs a hand over his jaw then pauses as if caught in mid-epiphany.

"Jack?" I ask, breaking him from his trance.

He grimaces. "I think I've got an idea."

\*\*\*\*

I can't sleep. The buzz from the good parts of the read-through has me amped up, while the badness and tension has plunged me into depressive insomnia. No amount of melatonin could even this out. The only thing that might calm my mind is a crystal ball with amazing reception. If I can just see how all of this is going to turn out, I'll be able to relax for two seconds.

But life, unfairly, doesn't work like that. At eleven-thirty, I give up on my relaxation hypnotherapy MP3 and go to my desk.

My novel is, as always, open on the desktop. I hardly ever turn off my computer, but I've restarted it at least three times since the convention, opened the file, and done nothing with it. I have the urge to work on it, now, but nothing comes.

I've wanted to write this stupid book for years, but I never have the time. It's always this screenplay, these revisions, that treatment, punch this up. When I do get some down time, I'm too exhausted to use my brain to actually write. Because who wants to do their job for free and fun?

There's also a little bit of embarrassment that I can't quite get rid of when I think about writing a book. I didn't set out to be a novelist. I've always wanted to write scripts. I started out with plays, because I understood the format. I moved on to screenplays when I recognized the limitations of staging a story. When I first began writing, I had a fantastic imagination, a gnawing hunger to put words on the page.

Now, I've been staring at a blinking cursor for five or six minutes every few days before slinking off without a thing written.

What happened to me?

I half-heartedly type a few lines, but it feels wrong. The heroine feels too much like me. Her life isn't interesting enough for anyone to want to read about it. And all of it is so heavy-handed.

With a noise of disgust, I push back from my desk and pace my bedroom. It's not just *Beautiful Darkness* sucking my soul out. It's everything. It's trying to play the game and get ahead. It's the sacrificing and compromising, and knowing that I'll never be the one benefiting from either of those actions.

It's knowing I've given up something I should have never given up, because the pay-off I sold myself out for is never, ever going to come.

It's remembering that stupid kiss.

My phone is in my hand before I can convince myself it's a bad idea. The call rings for so long that I begin to doubt he'll pick up. But after a day like today, there's no way he's asleep.

"Hey," he answers, his voice so soft I can barely hear him. "What do you need?"

What *do* I need? Nothing that I can ask for. "I don't *need* anything. I just couldn't sleep. I was thinking about the read-through today, and it's got me all freaked out and messed up."

"Right."

It's not like him to be so monosyllabic. Not with me. "And I just wanted to talk to someone about it. And I'm not on a call-at-almost-midnight basis with Marion."

"Uh-huh."

My brow furrows. "Did I do something wrong?"

"What? No." It's the first time his voice rises to a nearing-normal volume. "I just can't talk, right now."

The bottom of my stomach plunges. My chest hurts. Of course. Of course he can't talk. He's with Madison.

I squeeze my eyes shut. I will not imagine him standing just outside his bedroom, in that ridiculous little alcove he still can't figure out how to decorate, keeping his voice low so he doesn't wake her. Or maybe she's in the shower. Or slipping into something more comfortable.

Everything in me aches to try to keep him on the phone. To keep him from going back to her. But there's nothing I can do, and I have no right, anyway. So, I have to say, "Oh my god, I'm so sorry. I had no idea—"

"It's okay. We'll talk tomorrow," he promises, and hangs up.

I stare down at the phone in my hand in disbelief, then toss it across the area rug.

I still can't sleep, but now, it's because I'm imagining all the future headlines I'm going to have to endure. All the gossip and paparazzi sightings, and is that a baby bump? A ring on her finger?

All of this is my fault. I want him back. And, now, it's too fucking late.

June 4, 2011

Dan is a boom operator. He has curly sandy-blond hair that makes him look like a friendly surfer. It's our second date, and we spent it lying on the hood of his car, parked all the way out at a state park in the desert. He brought a picnic. He's earnest and sweet, and yeah, there's probably a lot of granola in his kitchen. But he's not so driven and career obsessed that he's going to try and control mine.

He's not Jack.

"Thanks for tonight," I say as he pulls to a stop outside my apartment. "I needed this."

Dan half-lifts his hand from the top of the steering wheel. "Thanks for trusting me enough to let me drive you into the desert alone at night." His laugh is dorky, but charming, in a way I wouldn't get tired of at the six-week mark.

I could really like this guy.

As he leans toward me for a kiss, my phone audibly buzzes in my purse.

"Wow, you're really popular tonight," he says, trying for humor. But my purse has sounded like a bag full of vibrators all night.

Anger flushes my face, and I'm glad it suits the situation we're in. I could just be blushing because I'm so turned on or something. I shrug helplessly. "Look, do you want to come inside?"

His crooked grin somehow doesn't look cocky, the way it would on other guys. "I would really, really like that."

"Great." I make a wait-one-minute finger and say, "Just stay here a sec. I'm going to step out of the car and call my friend. She's doing the whole nervous check-in thing."

"No worries."

I bet he has that printed on a t-shirt.

I swing my legs out of the car and close the door, and take a few steps away so my conversation won't be overheard. Because it's not any of my friends. Well, it is. Or not.

"What do you need, Jack?" I ask when he picks up.

"You weren't answering your texts. I was just worried. I know you were seeing that guy—"

"You knew I was on a date, so you kept texting me nonstop?" My jaw aches from clenching my teeth.

"Because I was worried."

"Okay, Edward. Or Jacob. Or who the hell ever was trying to keep that brown-haired girl safe." I rub my forehead. "We're not dating, anymore, Jack."

"I know we're not. I mean, I would like to think you wouldn't be on a date with some other guy if we were."

"Is there a reason for this call beyond, 'I don't want you to fuck this guy'?" I snap, then look over my shoulder. Dan is fiddling with the stereo and not looking up. I hope like hell he's not listening.

"That isn't my motive," Jack claims, but he's too defensive. I mean, the use of "motive" alone.

"I have to go, Jack. I'll call you tomorrow." I hang up, turn off my phone, and compose my face before I go back to the car. I motion for Dan to roll down the window and say, "Sorry about that. You wanna come in?"

He turns off the car and follows me to the door, saying, "You know, I think it's really great that you have someone who cares about you that much."

"It is." A headache is forming behind my eyes. Luckily, stepping into the apartment gives me an automatic change of subject. "So, this is my place," I say, flicking on the lights.

He whistles. "Wow, women's apartments are a lot nicer than men's." He nods to the large ochre vase standing under its own lighting on a recessed shelf. "If this were my place, that would be a huge bong."

God, it's good to laugh. It's good to not talk about business. Just being around Dan is good.

So, when he kisses me, again, I'm fine with that. And, when he pushes my jacket off my shoulders, I'm fine with that, too. I'm fine with the trail of clothes we leave on the way to my bedroom, and even though he doesn't have Jack's huge biceps and rock-hard abs, Dan is pretty fine, too. And, when he goes down on me for forty-five minutes, that is *more than fine*.

It's still the awkward kind of first-time sex, where you're not quite sure how to make everything work the way you're used to it working. Jack used to like me to pull his hair, when it was long enough to get ahold of, but when I do it to Dan, he laughs and says, "Easy, I don't want a bald spot." When we fucked, Jack always wanted me on top, but Dan is all about the missionary, and I don't mind the change of scenery.

When it's all over, I feel great. I don't ask Dan to stay, but I'm hopeful we'll do this, again. I can easily imagine spending weekends together, watching movies and snuggling up in bed and having morning-breath sex. That would feel normal. Way more normal than thirty-minute dates sandwiched between call times, or weekend getaways doubling as foreign premieres.

Okay, I could never see having the same sex life with Dan that I had with Jack. There was all this sweet, worshipful respect that, while nice, could get stale after a while. I liked being in charge of Jack. Tying him down and teasing him until he literally begged. Just because I don't get paid for it, anymore, I still love Domming. But, if that's not something Dan is into, I could probably cope. I could trade that for a real life and a real relationship, as opposed to what I had with Jack.

My good feeling that lasts until morning. My phone's light isn't blinking, and my heart plummets. I kind of hoped Dan would have at least texted me. Then, I remember I turned my phone off. I scramble to turn it back on, pushing my hair out of my face as I sit up. There *is* a text, and it *is* from Dan.

*I know it's not cool to text from your driveway, but I am.*

I giggle and cover my face.

The doorbell rings.

155

Holy shit. I check the timestamp on the text. He sent it early this morning, right after he left. But he can't be at the door, because he doesn't have a security pass for the parking garage.

*Son of bitch.*

I bolt out of bed and pull on my robe, tying the belt with a ridiculous amount of force. Muttering under my breath the whole time, I stalk to the door and jerk it open.

Jack stands on my doorstep with a cardboard tray bearing two tall cups. "Half-fat caramel mocha, extra shot?"

"What the fuck are you doing here?" I don't even try to be polite about it. Because there is nothing about an early morning ambush that inspires politeness.

He frowns like the question is ridiculous. "Bringing you coffee. Like a friend."

"A friend calls first. Especially when that friend knows their friend had a date the night before." I seethe.

Jack's eyes dart past me, into my apartment. "Oh, shit, is he still here? I didn't—"

"You knew." I fold my arms over my chest, blocking the door even more. "You came over here to see if he stayed the night."

"If I thought he'd stayed the night, I would have brought three coffees." He tries for a charming smile. "I'm not rude."

"Actually, yes, you are. You tried to c-block me last night; now, you're here at ass-o-clock in the morning—"

"It's eleven."

"It doesn't matter what time it is!" I shout so loud that, now, one of the landscapers is staring at us. I lower my voice. "Are you going to do this every time I have a date? Any time you have the feeling that I might be moving on with my life?"

Jack has the nerve to act like the affronted party. "I'm sorry, I didn't realize it was that serious."

"It's not serious. Not yet. But neither was whatever her name was that you were all over *Star Magazine* with two weeks ago. And you didn't ask my permission to do that!" I hate how much that still gets under my skin. The pictures had shocked me when I was in the checkout line, buying emergency tampons. It was like a one-two punch of all the stuff that sucked in my life that day.

"I never said you had to ask for permission," he protests. "I just want—"

"You wanted to know if I fucked him?" I throw up my hands. "Fine. I fucked him. And it was amazing. And I hope we're going to do it, again."

All the color drains from Jack's face. I hate that I feel even slightly sorry for him, because he did this. Whatever he's feeling, now, is on him. But I hoped we would be able to not do the awkward ex thing. I want us to be the different kind of friends-after-lovers. The kind that ends with one of us presenting the other a lifetime achievement award with a fond speech about all the good times we've had.

"This was a mistake." He takes a step back, looking uncertainly at the tray in his hands. "I shouldn't have—"

"You're right. You shouldn't have." The sunlight is too harsh and bright all of a sudden. I didn't even drink the night before. This is a rage hangover. "Look, let's keep our distance. Just for now. We need to get some space between us before we can do this without freaking out every time one of us goes on a date."

"Yeah." He gestures behind him. "I'll call you. Not today. Probably not tomorrow."

"Okay. I won't change my number." I don't want Jack out of my life. But I don't want him to the be the reason it never breaks out of his orbit.

He nods, his expression pained. Then, he quickly covers it and says, "Do you want the coffee?"

"No, thanks. I'm trying to cut back." Lie. I'm going to go inside and put my espresso maker through the worst morning of its life. But I don't want Jack to think he's done anything good here today.

He nods, again, and turns. I close the door. Almost. I watch through the crack as he heads toward the parking lot. He motions to the landscaping guy with his weed whacker and gestures to the coffee.

I shut the door in disgust. Ugh. Yet another person who's going to think of me as the bitch who's mean to Jack Martin.

I didn't ask him for my key back, but I don't examine the reason why.

## Chapter Nine

Jack's solution to our Lynn problem arrives to an early morning writing meeting. It's two days before principle shooting begins. Andi Nebauer sits, her recorder poised in front of her, observing us and taking notes as Marion, Lynn, and I try to work together as pleasantly as possible.

"There are already blind items flying around about problems behind the scenes," Jack warned us during a conference call yesterday. A call during which Lynn was wisely silent. "You get along, even if you want to kill each other. And you all have to compromise. Nobody in that room is digging her heels in for any reason. Compromise, Lynn, means not getting every damn thing you want." Jack spoke to her as though she were a child, which definitely bodes well for her attitude today. She's all smiles and graciousness toward us, but that won't last once we're out of Andi's earshot.

Nor will any of the changes we make, I fear. Though I'm not sure the reporter can see it, Lynn has arrived in passive-aggressive battle mode. And we're still stuck on the last freaking word of the movie.

"I just don't understand what's wrong with 'always'," Lynn complains.

"It just too associated with Harry Potter," Marion explains patiently, as though we aren't trapped in this argument for the thousandth time.

"But J.K. Rowling doesn't *own* the word," Lynn protests. "Besides, my book has outsold *Half-Blood Prince* everywhere except Brazil."

*Well done, Brazil.*

"I'm not sure sales figures are going to matter to audiences." Marion says, and dismisses the concern with a flick of the page. "But we can film it both ways and see what our test audiences think."

"Or we could get an outside opinion." Lynn smiles sweetly at Andi. "What do you think? Does 'always' sound too much like Harry Potter?"

Andi holds up her hands. "I'm just here to observe the creative process, not be a part of it." Her tone is firm, but she laughs, and that laugh is the doorway to further wheedling.

"Yes, but you watch movies and read books. What's your opinion, is all I'm asking," Lynn says with her most charming smile. "As a viewer, not a reporter."

Andi shifts uncomfortably. "All right. I would say yes, 'always' would take me out of the story, and I would think of Harry Potter."

"Really?" Lynn appears thoughtful.

Shrugging, Andi replies, "That's what I thought when I read the book."

A chill falls over the room like a death shroud.

Marion is quick to jump in. "You read the book?"

"Of course. I can't do a story without research." Andi flips a page in her notebook. "I actually have some questions about it, if you get time for a break."

"You're with us all day, right?" Marion asks.

Andi nods. "And compiling more questions every minute."

"Great." Marion glances back down at the script. "Okay, so 'always' becomes 'forever'."

Lynn laughs. It's meant to sound like a friendly one. It isn't. "Well, we'll see."

"Moving on," Marion says, chipper as an animated bird. "Lynn, you were still concerned that the coatroom scene had been removed?"

"Of course I'm concerned," she says with an exasperated sigh. "The coatroom scene was one of the most talked about."

Which was why I retained it in the screenplay. I think it's a mistake to remove it, but there's no way I'm going to take Lynn's side in anything.

"We're worried that it might be a little difficult to get past the ratings board," Marion explains. I've heard her reasons, but

I'm interested to hear how she explains it to Lynn. "If we switched it from anal, maybe, but we'd need some new dialogue—"

"I'll write it," Lynn says instantly, her gaze cutting to me.

Marion considers. "Send it to Jess. She can plug it back into the scene."

"Why don't I just rewrite the scene?" Lynn asks, as though she's offering to do us a huge favor.

Marion looks to me, as if to say, *This one is all yours.*

I sit forward in my chair, considering my language carefully. "Writing a screenplay isn't like writing a novel."

"Well, clearly not." Lynn laughs at the clearly ridiculous obviousness of my statement. She lifts the edges of a few pages and lets them fall. "But the format is right here. I'm sure I can muddle through, somehow. It can't be *that* difficult."

"The format isn't really the issue." If I had a penny for every time someone assumed that screenwriting was just an easier version of prose because all you had to do was stick dialogue in it, I would have a much bigger apartment. "There are other things that need to be considered—"

"I'll probably be writing the screenplay for the second movie, anyway," she interrupts loftily. "It'll be good practice."

"Oh?" Marion's lips purse.

Lynn pushes her reading glasses up on her head. "That's going to be a part of the contract. I've been through all of this. By the time we're finished, I'll be qualified." She glances over at me. "And who better than the creator to know exactly how to present the story? Honestly, I feel like Jack has wasted poor Jessica's time even having her here, when I could have just done all of this from the start."

This is going to be a long, long day.

\*\*\*\*

Andi approaches me when we break for lunch. Marion graciously ordered in for us, but I have to get out of that

161

fucking conference room and away from Lynn. Jack's plan to make her cooperative is failing spectacularly. On the surface, she's compromising, but it's always with that frozen expression that, coming from a mother, would mean "you're in big trouble when there are no witnesses."

"Hey, do you mind answering some questions over lunch?" Andi asks as we step into the hallway.

*No, I want to smoke the largest joint anyone has ever rolled, not just in L.A., but worldwide.*

But I tell her, "Sure," and actually sound like I don't want to leap from a window.

We take our pho to the patio behind the building and sit in the rattan armchairs there.

"So," Andi says. "Let's start with something easy. What has your experience adapting the bestselling novel of all time been like?"

"That's the easy question?" I shake my head. "Off the record? You were in that room. You know what it was like. On the record? It's been an interesting experience with a unique set of challenges. I'm grateful to have had this opportunity to learn and hone my craft."

Her mouth twists into a knowing smile. "Okay, but some people would say that your craft is pretty sharp already. You've been honored with three nominations for best original screenplay from the Writer's Guild, a Golden Globe nomination… The bulk of your work appears to be original. What made you want to adapt *Beautiful Darkness*?"

*The paycheck.* "It's good to shake yourself up, sometimes. I think we have this perception that adapting a screenplay isn't as hard or as much work as writing something original, but they're both a lot of work. They're just different kinds of work."

"It seems like this one, especially, is a lot of work. You guys will begin principle filming this week, but it seems like the script is still going through a lot of changes."

I nod. "It is. It definitely is. But, sometimes, that happens. There are some films that are cut and dry. You go through the revisions, you put the script through its paces, and by the time cameras are rolling, it's a done deal. But there are others where you're looking at revisions throughout filming."

"And is this going to be one of those movies?" Andi asks.

"I really fucking hope not," bursts from my mouth before I can think twice. There's no way that's not going to make it into the story. She's been given a lot of access to the production, and she's not going to leave out little details like the fact that the writer is pulling out her hair.

"Moving on," she says, and I breathe a sigh of relief that I won't incriminate myself further. "By all accounts, Jack Martin was instrumental in bringing *Beautiful Darkness* to the screen. You've collaborated a lot with him in the past. What motivated him to come to you for this project?"

"I think you'd have to ask Jack about his motivations." I manage to get the sentence out without sounding as insulted as I feel. This is the type of question I tried to avoid so hard when I was first starting out. The inevitable moment where it feels like I'm on trial for my romantic past with Jack. But I push through with my usual answer. "Once you've established a working relationship with someone and you know that your styles mesh, you want to keep working with them. You know the other person's process, you know their little ticks and what will and won't work for them. On a project like this, where time is a factor, that's important."

"When you say time is a factor..." Andi leaves the sentence open so I can elaborate.

"Obviously, we want to cash in on the popularity of the book before it fades." *Oh. Fuck.* I did not just say that, did I? Scrambling, I add, "Because you want that project to succeed, not just for the studio, but for Lynn, too."

"Some people would say she's succeeded beyond reasonable expectations." It's not clear if Andi is making a comment or asking a question with that. "Lynn Baldwin has been open about that fact that she based the character of Damian Bennett on Jack Martin. Do you think that influenced his decision to get involved? Was there maybe some hope there that he might play the part himself?"

"Not at all."

"Lots of fans, though?" Andi nudges.

"Yeah, of course there were a lot of fans who wanted to see that happen, but Damian Bennett is in his twenties, and Jack is not. And he's very much aware of that." I can't resist adding, "Honestly, the focus on that from the fans and from other people seems to make him uncomfortable."

Andi nods thoughtfully. "I guess I'm puzzled as to why someone like Jack Martin would be interested in developing such a controversial book into a film. BDSM and underground fighting and all that."

Why indeed? I think back to the reasons he gave me. Someone was going to make money off the book, so why not us? Maybe we could make it better, less sensationalized. None of that sounds like an enthusiastic endorsement of the source material.

But I can't think of anything beyond that.

My heart pounds, and my mouth goes suddenly dry. Why didn't I think of this to begin with? Of course, he would want to shape this movie himself. Of course, he would want me involved. It's entirely because he wants to make the BDSM representation more accurate and less dangerous, the way I tried to do in the screenplay.

"Again, that's something you'd have to ask Jack," I manage to say calmly. "This book has captured the interest of so many people around the world, it seems like common sense that it might grab a few people in Hollywood."

"You should be working the PR department," she says with a laugh. "You're not giving me much to sensationalize here."

I shrug. "There isn't much to sensationalize, I'm afraid. Business as usual."

"Well, I'm not hoping to get much more from Jack. I knew when he called me it's because he thinks I'm safe." Andi shakes her head and moves to turn off her recorder. "Oh, real quick here, while I've got you. There are some rumors that Jack was interested in the project because his girlfriend, Madison Avery, wanted to star in it. Is that true?"

I bristle not just at hearing Madison described as Jack's girlfriend, but at the idea that she would need to sleep with a producer to land a role. "Madison Avery is an incredible talent. I'm not sure what you're getting at it."

Andi holds up her hands. "Oh, no, I think I've created a misunderstanding here. I don't think this is a case of Jack Martin picking a specific project so he can run it like his personal casting couch. Everyone in town describes him as something of a Boy Scout. But it does seem odd that right after casting is announced, she's suddenly stepping out all over town with him."

"So, you're asking which came first, the chicken or the lay?" I curse inwardly. "I don't feel comfortable commenting on those specifics."

So, why, why, why do I add, "But I do know that he recommended her to the casting director specifically. You can infer what you like from that."

Andi nods with an approving smirk. "Okay. Well, you enjoy your lunch. I'm going to hunt down Lynn Baldwin."

"Good luck with that," I say. It's a normal thing to say to anyone who's worked on pre-production with her. Not such a great thing to say to a reporter.

But who am I kidding? Lynn will incriminate herself far better than I can.

\*\*\*\*

True to form, she does.

I'm on my way back to the conference room, stealing myself for the next big fight, when I pass Andi on her way in the opposite direction.

"Hey, aren't you sitting in on—"

"Nope." She shakes her head vehemently and keeps stalking purposefully down the hall.

I turn and catch up with her. "So, Lynn—"

"I'm done with that woman." Andi never breaks her stride.

"Hang on, hang on," I say when we reach the elevator. "She's terrible. Nobody knows that better than me." *And Marion, and Jack.* "I need to know what I'm walking into."

"You're walking into a god damn minefield." She hits the button multiple times.

"And you laid the mines for me?" I try to laugh.

Andi doesn't. She gets on the elevator and says, "Tell Jack I'm not his whipping boy. I'll be in touch."

The doors close as I stare, open-mouthed.

My legs feel like lead as I trudge back to the conference room. Already, I hear raised voices. Lynn is furious, shouting over Marion.

"...and I can't believe you stood there and let her speak to me that way!" Lynn is practically screaming. "Your job is on the line, you know." Spotting me in the doorway, she jerks her pointed finger in my direction. "Yours, too! All it takes is a single phone call to Jack—"

Marion tilts her head, like she's studying a painting. The painting in this case would be called "Still Life With Angry Tomato", because Lynn is so red it's alarming. Marion, however, is calm and collected. Because she—and I—know the truth. "Who do you think sent Andi here?"

"He obviously didn't know she was going to ask so many rude questions!"

"Probably not. But he thought she might keep you in line." Marion arches a perfect brow.

Lynn's nostrils actually flare. "Excuse me?"

"I don't think you realize how close you are to being shut out of this entire project," Marion goes on, and it's a shock to me, for sure. Because I thought the whole deal was ironclad, with no way of getting around Lynn's brilliant ideas.

"I have total creative control—"

"No," Marion interrupts her. "You have a lot of creative control. But not total. And Jack might baby you, but I'm not going to. You just got a deal for a second book. What's going to happen with your publisher if you act like a total nightmare and turn your fans against you?"

"My fans would never turn against me!" Lynn waves her arm around the room as though all of those fans are present. "I could walk outside, right now, and shoot someone in the street, and they would defend me."

"They probably would," I interject.

"Thank you," Lynn snaps.

I can't help myself. "It wasn't a compliment."

Before she can respond, Marion says, still calm and reasonable, "This is the reality, Lynn. You're hot shit, right now, but that won't last forever. If you make enemies, you'll probably get your second movie. You'll get more book deals. But, eventually, doors will close on you. There's always a tipping point. You need people on your side when you hit it."

Lynn says nothing in response. She snatches up her bag, and I'm wondering where Kathy is to carry it. Come to think of it, I haven't seen Kathy all day.

"I'll be talking to Jack about this," she warns finally, as she stomps toward the door.

"I bet you will," Marion calls after her, as Lynn shoulders past me.

I watch her stalk down the hall, her petal-pink cardigan flapping at her sides like the Wicked Witch's cape. "I suddenly understand where J.K. came up with Dolores Umbridge."

Marion doesn't laugh. Her hands shake visibly.

"Holy shit, are you okay?" I step inside and shut the door behind me. "You're like, trembling."

"I hate conflict." She braces her hands wide on the table and drops her head, taking a deep, audible breath.

Easing into one of the chairs, I ask, "What happened?"

"Andi made the mistake of asking about that damn fanfic." Marion straightens and exhales.

"Yikes." I feel like one of us should have warned her, somehow. "That was all it took?"

Marion nods, chewing the inside of her cheek. "It really set her off. She started in on how the studio should sue the writer for infringing on her property, and she was really disappointed that they hadn't issued a statement. It was all bullshit. But it was very loud bullshit."

I make a closed-lip, noncommittal noise.

We sit in a silence that isn't awkward so much as filled with despair.

"You know we're not going to be around for the sequel, right?" Marion says finally, with a grim chuckle.

"Thank god for that."

We both nod in agreement, with no idea where to go from here.

****

It's nine o'clock, and I'm on my couch, cuddled under a cashmere throw and binge-watching *Stranger Things*. One of the worst parts about working in entertainment is that there's so much you're expected to have seen. *Oh, you're a screenwriter? You've seen the new Batman, then, right? I'm watching this show on Amazon, right now, and oh my god, it's so good—but I'm sure you've already seen it.* The reality is, I'm usually so busy on my own work, I rarely have time to see anything that isn't required for some kind of voting.

As the end credits of the episode roll, I pick up my phone. I hate how hopeful I am, but I want to see a call from Jack that I've somehow missed when I was engrossed in Winona

Ryder's TV comeback. My ringer is on, and there are no missed calls. Not even to shout at me for the disastrous day.

Not that any part of the disastrous day was actually my fault. All of that can be dumped directly on Lynn.

*Unless Jack is so incredibly furious with you that he won't call you.*

I consider calling *him*, but we're going to meet in the morning, anyway. And the last thing I want is another of those awkward, "I can't talk right now", moments.

The phone buzzes in my hand, startling me. It's a text from Sherri.

*TSW. NOW.*

Sherri is addicted to "They Said What?", a media gossip blog. Either she's angry because she's on it, angry because she's not on it, elated because she's on it, or elated that she's not on it. Due to the confining nature of the written word via text, I can't tell.

I open the web browser on my phone. Of the fourteen open tabs, one of them is always TSW. I tap it and pull down to refresh.

It's a picture of Lynn, and walking an obedient two steps behind her, Kathy Muller. Kathy's face is circled in red.

*Breaking news from the set of* Beautiful Darkness: *author Lynn Baldwin appears to be the target of a new, anonymous memoir released over the weekend. The book,* She Swallowed Me Whole, *debuted on Amazon's self-publishing platform Sunday morning, but has already sold twenty-thousand copies in less than forty-eight hours. The story broke shortly after links to the book hit seemingly every major* Beautiful Darkness *fan site—and hate blog—on the internet. Readers didn't have to reach far to guess that the sordid tale of a demanding, suddenly famous author wasn't exactly fiction, and that the author, M. Deplume, is the most likely Kathy Muller, Lynn Baldwin's assistant.*

Holy shit.

That was why Kathy wasn't there today. Dollars to donuts.

*The book includes such scintillating details as the diva author, "Lauren Caldwell", throwing a tantrum after failing to wrangle an invitation to a star-studded charity ball and hiring tutors to do her children's homework. Deplume also characterizes the author as a demanding wife to a husband relegated to a nanny's role, and who may or may not be having an affair with Deplume herself.*

My phone rings this time, and I answer it without checking the number. I blurt, "Kathy Muller is dead," before I even consider that it might not be Sherri on the line.

"What?" Jack's startled exclamation jolts me to attention. "I'm getting dressed. Meet me at the office."

"Wait, wait," I say, before he can hang up. "She's not dead. I don't think she is, anyway. I thought you were Sherri."

He lets out a relieved breath I can hear over the line. "So, you saw the book?"

"I haven't seen the book. I saw an article about it."

"Fucking *TSW*." Most people in town hate that site, but Jack even more so, after they published pictures of him taking advantage of a nude beach at a Caribbean resort. "Did you have any indication today that Lynn knew about any of this stuff?"

"I did not. I mean, she was snippy, but she's usually snippy." I chew my lip. "You know, she did go, like, atomic on that reporter."

"So I hear." He groans. "Well, tomorrow's going to be an interesting day, isn't it?"

"There's an old adage about that, isn't there? A curse, or something? May you live in interesting times?"

"I don't think they were talking about this movie," he says dryly. "Then again, I wouldn't wish this experience on anyone."

I remember what Marion said earlier in the day. "You knew that Lynn stormed off during our rewrite meeting, didn't you?"

"No. Why didn't anyone tell me?" He sounds shocked and miffed. "I think that might have been one of the signs that something was wrong."

"Honestly? I just expect it at this point." My stomach sinks. "Marion said she and I wouldn't be attached for the sequel. Do you think that's true?"

"They still haven't optioned the next one. But she's lobbying hard to write it, when they inevitably do." He pauses. "I don't think she can pull it off. But come on. Do you really want to go through this, again?"

I don't. I won't care if I never see Lynn Baldwin, again. But I can't decide what's worse: not putting myself through the hell of the sequel, or giving her what she wants.

Excerpt: She Swallowed Me Whole

Lauren's obsession with this movie star dominated every conversation I had with her. I felt like she was just waiting for me to bring up something she could make all about him. She would spend whole days emailing me links to fanfic of his movies. I would always tell her that I read them, but I rarely did. I was not as interested in him as she was.

Then, one day, she sent me something of her own. "I wrote this for him," she wrote. "Do you think it is good enough to publish?"

I told her I would read it and get back to her, but the truth is, I have never read a single word of it. Not even now that it is a bestseller.

Jenny Trout

Chapter Ten

I have no idea where Kathy Muller went. Possibly she really is dead. Which is a shame, because I would very much like to buy her dinner.

Since "M. Deplume" started burning up the self-published bestseller chart, Lynn has been decidedly hands-off in the creative process, allowing Marion and I to revise the script as we see fit. Wren and Madison spent the first week of shooting getting all of those pesky sex scenes out of the way. Though Lynn originally tried to get permission to be on set for those, Jack didn't have to bother opposing her; for almost five whole days, Lynn has been radio silent.

Maybe it's cruel-hearted of me to revel in her humiliation the way I have. But it really does make my job a hell of a lot easier. All I have to deal with is the stupid coatroom scene, and I'll be blessedly finished.

I eat breakfast at home before I head to the studio, scrolling idly through Facebook on my phone as I finish my coffee. I'm so used to seeing gossip about *Beautiful Darkness* cross my feed, I barely blink at the headline below the picture of the stunning blond woman, until I realize that it's Lynn.

So, at least I know where Lynn has been for part of the time. Because when I open Andi Nebaur's article, entitled "Queen of *Darkness*?", I'm greeted by striking new photos of not just Lynn, but also Wren and Madison. The photographer has styled Lynn as some kind of sleek, modern empress in a black pantsuit. Her hair is up in a polished beehive, and she sits comfortably on an armchair that looks like a throne with its ridiculously high tufted back. Madison, in a silky red dress that spills over her body like a bloodstain, poses on a faux polar bear rug at Lynn's feet, while Wren crouches like a well-dressed loyal hound in his black suit and tie.

My gaze lingers on Lynn's face. There's no wonder she looks so comfortable in her pose. This is how she sees herself, and finally, we're all being forced to see her this way, too. She's not just comfortable. She's god damn triumphant.

I scroll down in disgust. Andi opens her piece with the usual explanation of what *Beautiful Darkness* is, who Lynn is, why it's becoming a movie, etc. I skim that section, down to the block letters at the beginning of a new paragraph. *The atmosphere in the writing room is tense. It's only noon, and tempers are flaring. Screenwriter Jessica Yates is best known for her original work, but she's viewing this adaptation as a new challenge. Over lunch, she will tell me, "I think we sometimes have this perception that adapting a screenplay isn't as hard or as much work as writing something original, but they're both a lot of work," but no one out of Baldwin's earshot would describe the author as easy-going. Yates and director Marion Cross are at an impasse with Baldwin over the final word of dialogue. The level of power Baldwin has been granted over the creative process isn't just unprecedented. It's a hindrance.*

*The problem, according to Baldwin's former assistant, Kathy Muller, is that Baldwin "thinks she's a big Hollywood player, now. She's always wanted to be important, so she's throwing her weight around and enjoying it."*

So, Andi tracked down Kathy. I wonder how many other entertainment journalists will. She better get an agent.

*Of everyone involved in the maelstrom of* Beautiful Darkness, *Muller is perhaps the one closest to the eye of the storm. Before Baldwin's meteoric rise to literary stardom, Muller was a regular Oklahoma girl herself. Related to Baldwin, somehow ("Who can keep all those once removed and second and thirds straight? We just say we're cousins."), Muller still owns her modest bungalow on the same Tulsa cul-de-sac where Baldwin and her family once lived. She'll be returning there soon.*

*"If you tell a person they're wonderful often enough, they start to take it upon themselves to say it for you," Muller demurs when asked if her resignation was acrimonious.*

There's no mention of *She Swallowed Me Whole*, but further into the conversation with Kathy, Andi writes:

*I ask Muller if the recent allegations that* Beautiful Darkness *shares similarities and an uncanny amount of text with "Darkness Standing", a fan fiction story inspired by Jack Martin's movie,* Last Man Standing, *have any merit. "I wouldn't know. I've never read either of them."*

My phone rings. It's Sherri. I answer.

"Are you reading it?" she asks, a note of mean glee in her voice.

"Don't have too good a time with it. This is my life, you realize?" And it has been plunged into soap opera-worthy drama.

"Call me when you're finished."

I promise I will and hang up the phone to return to the text.

*Cristin Zavada-Welch, who authored "Darkness Standing" under the online pseudonym MollyCuddles94, declined to speak about the issue directly, but her lawyer informs us that his client is "exploring all avenues available". To what end remains unclear.*

My curiosity is satisfied for the moment. I take a few calming breaths, then text Sherri. *Can't deal with any of this, now. Will call when I get back from meeting.*

I'll have more to tell her by then, anyway.

\*\*\*\*

Lynn stares me down across the table. I haven't finished reading the article, but I can only assume I've been quoted saying something far worse than I remember saying, to inspire that face.

Marion sits across from me. The gaze she fixes on Lynn sends a clear message: *if you want to make eye contact with me, I won't look away first."*

If Andi thought the writer's room was tense before…

Lynn finally breaks her glare from me to look down at the notebook in front of her. "I would like to know," she begins slowly, every word clipped and tense, "why I received a new draft of the script with the coatroom scene restored."

"We talked about that at our last meeting," Marion reminds her. "You wanted it added back in, and I said it would have to be a version that will still get by with an R-rating."

"And I told you I would rewrite it." She stabs her finger into the script so hard it looks painful.

"And we told you that we needed those changes as soon as possible," I remind her. "Marion called you. I emailed you. You never returned any of those. Were we supposed to hold up production of the entire movie while we waited for you to deliver the pages you volunteered to write?"

"I don't know if you're aware, but I am between assistants at the moment." Lynn speaks through lips pursed so tightly it looks like her whole face will be sucked into the event horizon of her mouth. "I did not have a chance to look at—"

"Wait a minute." I can't quite believe what I'm hearing. "It's somehow my fault that you didn't check your email?"

"This is *my* movie!" Lynn shouts, slamming her palms flat on the desk and pushing herself from her chair with a loud clatter. "And I made it quite clear that nothing was going into it that I did not write."

"Everybody just calm down," Marion tries, but it's too late. The seal has been broken, and all of our anger is pouring out like demons from the mouth of Hell.

Lynn jabs her finger at me, her hair swinging against her face and catching at the corner of her mouth. "I don't know what sick obsession you have with trying to take my book from me, but it's increasingly pathetic. I might even have to take out a restraining order against you!"

"Whoa." Marion holds out both hands, as though either of us might lunge for each other at any moment. "This is out of hand."

"You had the chance to write the scene, Lynn," I remind her. "But you chose to play a control freak game, instead. I don't even see what it matters to you when you ripped off the god damn book in the first place!"

Her hand moves so fast I don't realize she's thrown the water glass until it connects with my forehead. I crumple immediately, my eyes snapping shut instinctively. I can barely hear anything over the throb of pain, but Marion is shouting for security loud enough that it gets through. It's muffled, but I also hear her yell, "Don't you move a fucking muscle, Lynn." Maybe she's not yelling. Maybe it's because Marion is at my side, helping me sit up. When I open my eyes, something drips into them.

"Stay with me, now," Marion urges me, like I lost a whole arm, instead of getting dinged in the face with a water glass. But she's right, I'm starting to fuzz in and out.

After that, things get a little hazy. I know there's an ambulance ride, but I hear someone direct them to take me to a clinic the studio sends workman's comp claims to, so I'm not ER-worthy. That makes me feel better. I think I throw up in the back of the ambulance, or maybe I just feel like I'm going to.

I know one thing for sure: that was the last time I'll see Lynn Baldwin.

\*\*\*\*

Jack meets me at the clinic, a studio lawyer right behind him as they enter my cubicle. I'm sitting on the cart, legs up, head leaned back. It feels stupid to be propped up like a patient on an episode of ER, but I almost fainted while they were stitching me up.

"Holy cow. She really did a number on you," Jack says with a low whistle.

"Let's refrain from making statements like that," the lawyer advises.

A muscle ticks in Jack's jaw. He gently pushes my hair back from my face, his eyes never leaving the cut. "I'm saying that as her friend, not a representative of the studio."

"I suppose you guys are here to tell me what my options are? To offer me something so that I don't go rogue on Instagram? So I don't press charges against that bitch?" I'm too tired to do any of those things, right now. My head is killing me, and all I want is a painkiller. Which is probably why the studio has ambushed me with a lawyer, now, when I'm still in shock.

A grown woman threw a glass at my head. A grown woman, having a temper tantrum.

Jack straightens and puts his hands on his hips, pushing back the lapels of his jacket. "I wanted to check on you. They wouldn't let me without bringing him along."

"To make sure you didn't promise me anything." I lower my head, every pulse behind the wound causing further agony. "I could press charges, you know. This is assault."

"It was," Jack says.

"We're not calling it assault," the lawyer corrects him quickly. I hate this guy. His teeth are too tall, his hair too blond. Someday, he'll run for state senate on an extremely conservative platform, I can guarantee it.

"As her friend, I'll call it whatever I want," he snaps. "Can you just give her your card and take a hike?"

The lawyer sighs deeply, fishes in his jacket for a card, and hands it to me. "We're going to set up a meeting with a mediator and get this settled. For now, I have a non-disclosure you need to sign." He rests his briefcase near my feet and pops the locks to produce a multi-page document with flags sticking off the edges. "This is standard. You're not to speak to the media. No magazines, no blogs, definitely no paid interviews.

And you don't press any charges until we're able to work on this internally."

"Is it even legal to tell me not to go to the police?" I snatch the pages from him.

"Anything can be legal if you throw enough money behind it." That charming smile, again.

I shoot a glare at Jack. "This is bullshit, and you know it."

"Yeah, well, there's a lot of bullshit going around."

What the fuck does he mean by that?

It doesn't matter. If I'm being bullied into signing some stupid agreement, that's what I have to focus my attention on. "I hope you've both got some time, because I'm reading this whole thing."

"I would never suggest that you shouldn't." The lawyer's shark-toothed smile widens.

There's nothing nefarious looming in the pages, aside from how generally nefarious it is to ask an assault victim to keep things on the hush-hush so her assailant won't face bad publicity. As I initial pages and scribble my signature, my anger fades into numb complacency. There won't be any consequences for her over this. I don't make Macrocosm the kind of money she will.

"I want it noted by both of you that I will no longer work with Lynn in person. If there are any changes that need to be made, Marion can—"

Jack winces. "That's something we actually need to discuss. Privately." He shoots the lawyer a pointed look.

Great. I'm getting fired.

The lawyer takes his time checking to make sure every I is crossed and every T is dotted. Eventually, a nurse comes in with a Dixie cup of water and some Tylenol. I resist my urge to ask her for some Valium, as well. I just want Jack to tell me that they're removing me from the project so I can go home and work out my emotions on a box of wine.

"Well, human resources and legal will probably both be in touch with details on the personal protection order." The lawyer says as he snaps his briefcase closed.

"Don't I have to press charges for that?" I ask.

"It's not for you. It's against you." The lawyer at least has the good sense not to smile at that. "Ms. Baldwin feels unsafe."

"*She* feels unsafe?" Considering the way I feel at the moment, maybe she should.

The lawyer ignores me. "Jack, I assume you remember what you are and are not authorized to say as a representative of the studio?"

"I'm not an idiot, John."

It only now occurs to me that the guy didn't even bother to introduce himself to me. That, more than anything, tells me exactly who the studio is backing.

Lawyer John leaves, and Jack stands silently for a few seconds, clearly waiting to make sure the guy has really gone. He steps to the curtain and pulls it back, peeking out to check, before turning to me and asking, "What the hell happened?"

I hold up my hands. "Lynn went off the grid for like a week, so Marion had me write the coatroom scene."

"She threw a glass at you over that?"

"She threw a glass at me because I said that she ripped off the story." That doesn't matter. She still shouldn't have physically assaulted me. And Jack will feel the same.

"That's not an excuse. But, wow, you picked a bad time to needle at her over that." He rubs his hand over the back of his neck. "MollyCuddles94 filed today."

"No!" Even though it's the direct cause of me getting glass in my head, I'm thrilled to hear it. Something has to take Lynn down. If there's any justice in the world, something will go wrong for Lynn. "She's suing?"

"I don't know all the details, yet. Right now, the only defendants named in the suit are Lynn and her publisher, so I know zilch." He frowns. "Didn't you read the article?"

"I read part of it," I say, like a kid giving an excuse for not doing the homework. "I was in a rush to get stabbed in the head with jagged glass today. All I read was the part where she interviewed me."

His expression falls. "Yeah, well. There was more than one part about you."

The air conditioning must have come on, because there's a definite chill in the room. "What are you talking about?"

"I hate to do this here," he begins. "But I have to say it, because the longer I go without saying it, the angrier I am. And I've been trying to figure out a way to say it that doesn't hurt you. I don't want to do that. But you hurt me."

I frown, really hoping this isn't about Lynn losing control. If he blames me for that—

"I read what you said about Madison. And I thought better of you."

My brain races. "I don't remember talking about Madison."

"I don't think Andi would have written it if you hadn't said it." He fishes in his pocket for his phone. It doesn't take him any time at all to find the article, which means he's had it pulled up all day, just waiting to talk to me about it. My heart plummets as he reads, "'When asked, Yates was the only member of the creative team willing to address rumors that Martin's new relationship with Avery had anything to do with him taking on producer duties. 'So, you're asking which came first, the chicken or the lay? I don't feel comfortable commenting on those specifics.' But, she adds, 'I do know that he recommended her to the casting director specifically. You can infer what you like from that.'"

My eyes widen, and what blood I have left rushes from my face. "No, no, Jack, it was *not* like that—"

"It's kind of hard to see how it could be any other way."

"I would never say anything like that to hurt your feelings. She put me in a weird spot," I protested. It feels weak even to me.

He puts his hands in his pockets. "Come on. You've been here long enough. And you're a writer. You know the importance of language. You should have said, 'I can't comment on that.'"

"I kind of did." It's hard to explain with a pounding headache. "It sounded so clever and not nefarious when I said it out loud."

Jack sits beside me on the cart, slouching. "See, the thing is, when I read that, I recognized it. I knew the tone of your voice. I knew how you would have said it if you'd been saying it to me, and that it would have been just a joke. But you weren't saying it to me. You were saying it to a reporter. Behind my back."

"I know, and—"

"Do you, though?" He won't look at me. "You know me. And you know how I feel about people talking about my personal life. That was really unfair."

"I'm sorry. That's all I can say. I fucked up, and I'm sorry, and I really hate that I've hurt your feelings like this." I pause. "And I don't want you to think that I'm criticizing your dating choices or anything."

"You're not?" A smile touches the corners of his mouth.

"Not at all." I don't know why, but I have the urge to scoot away from him a little. There's nowhere to go. "We've been through this together before. And we've always said that if we needed to alter our arrangement or end it, we would both be okay with that."

He nods thoughtfully, then meets my eyes. I can see it in his face; he doesn't have to say anything. But he does. "I have to make a choice between being your sub and being with Madison. And I choose Madison."

It's too much. My head hurts. My heart hearts.

"I want a real relationship," he goes on. "Not some weird in-between. I'm getting too old for friends with benefits."

"I get that. I do. And, if you want to end things with me, that's fine. But you can't…" My voice scrapes to a dry halt.

"Can't what?" he prompts.

"You can't come back if this thing with Madison doesn't work out. Or with the next one. If we're doing this, it's permanent." God, it feels terrible to say that. A part of me threatens that giving up Jack is going to be giving up my last shot. I'll never be with anyone, again. But intelligently, I know that Jack is the reason I haven't been with anyone else, at least, not seriously.

"I don't think I will," he says, and he can't possibly know how crushing a blow it is. I would rather have been hit in the face with another water glass. That was so much less painful. He stands, and the small distance between us feels like a slamming door. "What we had for these last few years was fun, and it made us feel good. But it hasn't been healthy. We haven't moved on. And that's my fault."

We're equally culpable, but I don't want to admit that.

I ask, "So, this thing with Madison. This is serious?" and observe carefully. If there's even a flicker of doubt, either in the way he words his answer or in his expression or tone of voice, I'll know that it's now or never. If I see an opening, I'll tell him everything. That I've never stopped loving him, that I was stupid to break up with him years ago, that I refused to move on and was grateful that I didn't have to. And, if I don't get that opportunity, that's it. It's over.

His "Yes," is immediate and unflinching.

How, in so short a time, can it be serious? I want to laugh at him and argue, but that wasn't the deal I made with myself, and it would be pathetic and grasping.

But how? How could he be with me for so long, then instantly fall for someone else? *But he wasn't with you. He was fooling around with you.* And that's my fault. I was the one who set those limits and demanded he settle for them.

"You're happy." I don't add a conditional. No "if" or "as long as". "That's what I care about. If you can't be happy in our current arrangement, I wouldn't be very happy, either. And I wouldn't be a very good friend."

"You know, you're the only ex I've ever actually been able to stay friends with?" he asks, something sad in his voice. I wonder if he regrets not staying friends with the others, or if he regrets that I'm an ex. Hopefully, he doesn't regret staying friends with me.

"Yeah, well. Maybe that's not a comment on me so much as on the quality of your exes," I try to joke, but it falls painfully flat. "Look, I've been thinking about something, too. Not us related. Not really."

"Oh?" He seems relieved at the change of subject.

I take deep breath. "I need some time away. I know we talked about that crime drama—"

"You don't need to make a decision on that, right now," he interrupts.

"I've already made my decision. This thing with Lynn… I don't know if I ever want to write another movie, again." I blow out a frustrated breath. "When I started writing, it was because I loved it. Now, it's a job. And it's a job I'm grateful for. I'm never going to not be grateful to you for giving this to me. But I need to take some time to figure out what's next."

The perpetual furrow in his brow deepens. "Do you want to direct or something?"

"I want to finish my novel," I admit, though it's been a somewhat sore subject in the past, with Jack insisting that the only point in writing a novel is to see it end up on the screen, and me accusing him of never reading anything but press releases.

To my surprise, he doesn't give me crap about it. Not even in a joking way. "I think, after this, you've earned a break."

His phone buzzes, and he looks conflicted.

"Go back to work, Jack," I tell him. "Sherri's going to pick me up. She's probably on her way, right now."

"Okay. I'll call you tonight."

When he's gone, the nurse enters with some paperwork and print-outs about head injuries. She has light brown skin and a slight frizziness to her pulled-back salt-and-pepper hair, and the sympathy in her expression makes her look like she could be someone's favorite coworker. Noting my red-rimmed eyes, she asks, "Are you okay?"

I sniffle miserably. "My head just really, really hurts."

She purses her lips, as though I just confirmed something she's suspected all along. "I'm going to talk to the doctor. See if we can't get something stronger than Tylenol."

"That would be great," I rasp.

If it works for headaches, it will probably work for heartache, too.

February 3, 2012

This time, I'm the one sitting in the passenger seat, having my heart broken.

"You're not over him," Dan says gently. He's not trying to hurt me. And deep down, I know he's right.

But I lie, anyway. "If anyone is having a hard time getting over anyone, it's Jack. But he's just a friend, I swear."

"I know you're not sleeping with him behind my back or anything like that. I don't think you're that kind of person. But come on, Jess. Would you be happy in a relationship with someone knowing that they're always going to come in a package deal with someone who's not over them?"

I don't have an answer for that. Because as I sit here with this sweet, caring guy, all I can think about is how boring my life would be without Jack in it. Dan and I don't have that much in common. I can't imagine trading my friendship with Jack for hikes, visiting farmers' markets and playing Frisbee golf on Saturdays. Because Jack and I really are friends. We work in the same part of the industry, know the same people, go to the same parties.

And no matter how much I thought I needed the exact opposite of Jack, it turns out that the exact opposite of Jack is also the exact opposite of me. I need middle ground, and Dan isn't it.

We break up amicably. It's not like we had a ton of time invested in each other. We've only been exclusive for three months. It's still a bummer. I call Sherri, she promises to come over, and then, I get a glass of wine and have a good cry.

When Sherri arrives about an hour later, she immediately hugs me tighter than any hug she's ever given me before.

"Are you okay?" she asks. "I know I asked on the phone, but this was just out of nowhere. I'm shocked."

"It's not *that* out of nowhere," I lie. I had no idea it was coming. I just don't want to admit that I know how it feels, now, to be the person who got blindsided.

"Bullshit. If you'd seen this coming, you'd have told me." Sherri doesn't sugarcoat things. "Did he tell you why?"

"Yeah. It's…" I hesitate. Sherri has warned me before about Jack. I don't want to prove her right. "Okay, it was about Jack."

"What? About how the two of you are still both totally in love with each other?" She arches a brow. "Yeah, I would have a hard time dating someone in that situation, too."

My jaw drops. "Excuse me, but I am not still 'totally in love' with Jack. At least, not romantically. I love him as a friend."

"As a friend?"

"Yeah. A friend." I shouldn't sound this defensive. But I shouldn't have to defend myself, either. "We hang out, sometimes. We don't hate each other. And we don't have sex."

"Right, because the only way you can be in romantic love with someone is if you have sex with them." Sherri folds her arms. "I have never seen two people so deeply in denial."

"Look, you don't have to understand what's going on with Jack. But Dan should have. I mean, he would have. If he trusted me," I protest. "I'm not going to cheat on him with Jack."

"Maybe it isn't about trust," Sherri suggests. "What if— and I know this sounds crazy—but what if he wanted to be someone's first choice? And not just the guy who replaced the one that got away."

"Jack didn't get away. I let him go," I remind her. "But you have a point. I probably wouldn't be comfortable dating a guy who was best friends with his ex."

"Excuse me!" Sherri puts her hands on her hips. "I thought I was your best friend."

"You can have more than one. This isn't middle school. But, if it makes you feel better, I could always buy you one of those bracelets.

"Oh, could you, please? They're so fashionable." She laughs and drops her arms. "Or you could braid me one and put lettered beads on it."

"The last time I had one of those, it said PLUR on it." I wince. "I have kind of an embarrassing rave past."

"Well, I'm not going to tell you how to live your life." That's a sign that Sherri is about to tell me how to live my life. "But it's never going to be fair of you to put Jack before whoever you're dating. And, if you find a guy who'll put up with that, then congratulations, you've found a doormat."

"That seems a little judgmental of my hypothetical future boyfriend," I point out.

She shrugs, her expression a study in non-apology. "I'm judgmental. Everyone has flaws."

Talking about a breakup gets boring after a while, so Sherri and I decide to head to the Pilates class I was going to skip. It'll give her a chance to check out the studio I've been trying to get her to go to for ages. It's a new one that's just opened up in the space beside the sushi restaurant where Jack and I, sometimes, have lunch.

After class, Sherri points out the restaurant. "Do you ever go to that place?"

From here, I can see the table by the window where Jack and I usually sit. Is that weird, that we have our own "place"? Do exes-turned-friends do that?

I shake myself out of my thoughts and lie, "No. I've never been there."

"Do you want to try it? I'm starving." Sherri asks, jerking her thumb in the direction of the door.

"No. I need something more substantial than rice and raw fish."

And I want something secret, something that belongs between just Jack and me.

## Chapter Eleven

Park City, Utah in January is rough on someone who's lived in—and rarely left—L.A. for the past fourteen years. I bounce on the balls of my feet, numb despite the fleece-lined boots that I will never wear, again, after this week because I'll be god damned if I ever go anywhere with an average temperature of less than forty degrees Fahrenheit, ever again.

Beside me, Sherri is rosy cheeked and cheerful. It's day four, and her movie has already screened, to massive acclaim. She sparkled at the Q & A that followed. The press loves her, and she loves them. I feel like I've seen my best friend go from "actress" to "star" in one night. And while I'm beyond proud of her, she's not "do you know who I am?" famous enough to bypass the line at restaurants, yet.

"I love you," I say, finally breaking into her exuberant chatter about how good the desserts are at this place. "And I love tiramisu. But I've been freezing all day. Can we just go back to the hotel and do room service?"

She makes a face. "Really? You want to hole up in the room when all of this—" she gestures wide at the bustling street around us "—is going on?"

"No. Yes." I feel like a total jerk for not wanting to hang out, but I'm wiped out and fighting what's become a chronic depressive episode.

I hate being the woman who mopes and mopes over a guy for months. I really do. And it has been months. Two of them. In that whole time, Jack and I haven't had lunch or called each other or texted. He liked something I posted on Facebook once, and that was it. In two months.

I'm not going back to the hotel because I'm sad and rejected. I'm just exhausted from *feeling* sad and rejected.

"I'm just really tired," I try, again. "And we have that party tomorrow night. I don't want to be too tired for that."

"Ooh, too true," Sherri concedes. "We're not spring chickens, anymore, huh?"

"Not at all." I nod toward the door. "I feel bad depriving you of fantastic dessert. Especially on your fitness vacation."

"We can hit this place tomorrow," she says, blowing it off. If Sherri can say that about dessert, then I know for a fact she's not bothered by skipping it. "Besides, I'm freezing my tits off out here."

My mood lifts as we walk toward the shuttle stop and the prospect of a hot bath and a warm robe. Our room is small, but it has a gas fireplace that we've been toasting our feet in front of every night.

"You know, I really like the festival," Sherri says thoughtfully as we wait in the shuttle line. Because everything has lines here. "But I'm not sure I could do this every year."

"I'm going to need, like, a week in bed after this," I agree. "Sherri!"

A few steps down the sidewalk, a tall dark-skinned man in a sleek wool coat waves at us and jogs our direction. He's got a salt-and-pepper beard, a navy-blue fisherman's hat on, and a smile that's just for Sherri.

Though if she notices that last part, I can't tell. She seems almost indifferent when she says, "Oh, Davis. Hi."

Davis. The name rings a bell, but it takes me a moment to recognize him as the star of *Maui P.D.*. I'm used to seeing him in Hawaiian shirts and sunglasses. His show is on the same network as Sherri's. It's a quirky cult-favorite single-camera comedy that's won him at least one Emmy.

"Where are you heading?" he asks her, his gaze flicking to me. He holds out his hand. "Hi. Davis Andrews."

"Jessica Yates." My thick wool mitten feels kindergarten-ish in his black leather glove. How the hell does someone look so cool when it's so cold?

"We're headed back to the Astoria. Too much fun for one day," Sherri tells him. "What about you?"

"I'm trying to get fed tonight, but my chances are looking slim." He looks up and down the street, but his eyes quickly find Sherri, again. "Have you already had dinner?"

"No," I answer, before Sherri can. "And she's starving. I'm the one being a party-pooper."

"Why don't you come with me?" he suggests. "My friends are on the slopes, and there is no way I'm putting on skis. Not after the last time."

Sherri's smile widens. "What happened the last time?"

The shuttle pulls up, brakes squeaking. "How about I head back to the hotel, and he tells you his tragic ski story over dinner?" I look to him for backup in convincing her. Sherri can be reserved with people she doesn't know super well, and though I know she's met him a few times, she's never expressed any strong feelings, either way. He's clearly got some feelings about her, though, and holy cow, if a guy this hot is interested in her, I'd be a bad friend not to encourage it along.

"I don't know," Sherri says uncertainly. "I don't want to abandon you, Jess."

"I'm a big girl. If you're not ready to call it a night, it's fine with me." That gives her an out. That's a term of our friendship: always give each other an out. She can still say she's too tired and ask him for a raincheck, or she can consensually ditch me and go have fun. And I really hope she has fun. I want the whole week to be magical for her.

"If you're sure," she says, seeming genuinely concerned.

The line to get on the bus is shuffling forward. It's do-or-die time for Sherri, and we've been friends long enough to tell which way she's leaning. She hasn't taken a step to close the gap between her and the person in front of her, and she's moved significantly closer to Davis. Her shoulder is almost touching his arm.

"I'm fine. Seriously," Some alone time won't be too bad, anyway. Sharing a room with someone makes masturbating difficult, and it's been four days. "And I'm not trying to get rid of you, I promise."

"No, no, I don't think that at all," she assures me as I get swept forward in the line she's conspicuously excused herself from. "Text me when you get there, okay?"

If dinner is going horribly, she can always use my text as an excuse to bail. *Oh no, Jess has a really bad headache, and she needs me to bring back some Motrin.*

"I will," I promise.

"Okay. I'll see you back at the hotel," she says, pointing two fingers at me as I follow the line. "You're a good friend."

I smile to myself as I climb onto the shuttle. I feel like I've done a good deed for the night.

By the time I reach the hotel, I've warmed up a little. Not my feet, but those might have to be amputated, anyway. I slog into the lobby and pull off my fuzzy wool hat. The static electricity raising my hair is palpable. I don't care, even when I pass a group of toned, tanned skiers looking camera ready fresh from the slopes. *Thank God someone is doing the work of looking beautiful, because it's certainly not my job.*

That cheers me up a bit. Remembering that I can work in yoga pants most days is always a mood lifter.

"Jess?"

That mood crashes on take off at the sound of Jack's voice.

I try to push some of the hair that has attacked my mouth out of the way as I turn. "Hey! I didn't know you were going to be here."

"I didn't, either." He looks so good in his ribbed black sweater with the collar unzipped just-so. "But I found out Fernando was coming, so I thought what the hell? I haven't seen him in ages."

"So, you're here on business, not pleasure?" I ask, trying to sound arch and failing. "No, scratch that. You're here on pleasure—"

"Not business. Yeah." He smiles at me the way he does when I'm being a doofus. Affectionate and condescending at the same time. "You here for Sherri's movie?"

"Yeah."

"Right. I heard that went well." He clears his throat nervously. "Pass along my congratulations."

"I will." We stand there in silence for an uncomfortably long moment. There has to be something I can say to him. He's my friend, for god's sake. But all I really want is to ask is if Madison is here with him, and my throat seals off. I manage to say, "So, are you staying here?" at the exact same time he asks, "Have you hit the slopes, yet?"

We laugh and avoid eye contact.

"No," he says. "I was supposed to meet Fernando here for a dinner reservation, but so far, he's a no-show."

"Ah." I can't help but notice that he hasn't said, "we", yet.

*Stop it. You're embarrassing yourself.* And this *is* humiliation, of the most excruciating kind. Jack and I are both trapped in it, trying to be normal, failing horribly.

Something like resignation comes over him, and he says, "Look, this is weird. Which is stupid, because it should have been weird a long time ago."

"It *was* weird a long time ago." I shake my head ruefully. "But we're both weird people, Jack."

"Speak for yourself." Now that we have verbal confirmation of how fucking uncomfortable this meeting is, it doesn't seem as uncomfortable, anymore. He's the Jack I'm used to when he gestures toward the restaurant and says, "You wanna get something to eat?"

"Ugh, I just bailed on Sherri's dinner plans." I would feel like a tool if she came back and there I was, cheating on her with a different friend. But, if I told her how strange the whole encounter was and how I just wanted to get through it, she would understand, right? "But, yeah, as long as you have a reservation. I'm up for anything I don't have to wait in line for."

The Waldorf Astoria's restaurant is called Powder, which is so obvious as to be eye-roll worthy. The orange leather chairs and cushioned booths seem dated and modern at the same time, like we're eating in a 3D rendering of a Wes Anderson movie. The hostess suggests an intimate corner booth, and we both immediately object, opting, instead, for a table that feels like it's in the way in the center of the floor.

"So," I begin after the hostess has left us with our menus and the waiter has stopped by for our drink orders. "How's *Beautiful Darkness*?"

"Principle shooting got slightly behind because of the—" He gestures at my forehead, where my cut has healed into a thin, red scar. "Marion didn't want to come back at all."

"I don't blame her." I didn't. I got a call from Marion the day after the fight. She'd been ready to quit, and even threatened to file a restraining order against Lynn, but in the end, she'd stayed on the project. "Any consequences for Lynn?"

Jack's expression grows somber. "I'm sorry, Jess. I did fight for you. You probably don't believe that, but I swear, I wanted her banned from the set as much as you and Marion did."

"No, I believe you." I've never seen Jack get steamrolled by anybody before, and I doubt he'd lay down over something like this. "Is she causing any more trouble?"

"Let's see… Demanding her own trailer on set. Wanting fresh cut flowers delivered every morning? You know, the usual stuff she thinks everyone important asks for." He sounds beaten down. "I'm thinking you're right. I might never want to make another movie, again."

"That's just the fatigue talking," I reassure him. "This isn't the first time you've gotten burned out."

"It's the first time I've ever seriously considered changing my name and fleeing L.A.," he quips, then leans back as the waiter returns with our drinks. Even though it's eight o'clock, Jack is going to swill coffee. He's so charmingly addicted to it.

We place our orders, then I remember that I've left Sherri hanging. "Oh, shoot. Hang on, I have to text Sherri."

"About your change of plans?"

I shake my head, already tapping out a message. "Kind of? I'm letting her know I'm at the hotel. She's out with someone. If I text her, she can claim that it's an emergency or something."

"You guys really do that?" Jack's eyes widen. "Jesus, I thought that was just a T.V. thing."

"It's a safety and togetherness thing." I shrug and hit send. "I don't think she's going to use this out, though. She seemed into the guy."

"Who is it? Anyone I know?"

"You probably know *of* him. Davis Andrews? Super hot black guy," I hold my hand way above my head, "about yay tall. Has that T.V. show about cops in Hawaii?"

"Yeah, I know who that guy is. That show is terrible, but he's great. He read for something recently. Fuck, I have no short-term memory, anymore. What about you? Are you seeing anybody?" he asks, shaking a sweetener packet into his coffee.

"No." I pay very close attention to my silverware. "Not right now."

"Come on, Jess," he chides. "How long has it been since you went on a date?"

*Three years.* "I don't know."

He frowns in concentration. "It was, uh, that heart surgeon, right? The guy with the Alfa Romeo?"

I clear my throat.

"That was, like, years ago." He chuckles to himself as he stirs the spoon around his mug. The tiny clinks pelt me like barbed hail. "Dude. It's time."

It's the "dude" that does it. I'm suddenly thrust into the cold, harsh reality of knowing that I'm never going to be anything more than an ex-turned-friend to him. And all my fucks evaporate. "No. I'm still kind of hung up on someone."

He doesn't get the hint and lifts his mug for a sip. "What? Since when?"

"Since 2009, actually." I study his expression but keep my own blank. He stares back at me quizzically, and I see the exact moment he solves the puzzle.

"Are you…" He puts his mug down and swallows like someone experiencing heartburn. "Are you saying that I'm…"

"Yeah." I shrug and try to play it off with a laugh. "As it turns out, I never really got over you. Or wanted to break up with you in the first place."

I don't know what reaction I expected, but it sure isn't the one I get. "Are you fucking kidding me?"

My heart plunges into my stomach.

"All these years, and you never thought to say anything? It never once occurred to you—"

"No, it occurred to me. But you were already in a relationship, so I thought it was better this way." I maintain my calm, though the tone of his voice and the look on his face make me want to burst into tears.

"You thought it was better to let me go for—what, five years? Six?—without telling me that you still had feelings for me?" He says it like I've tricked him. He lowers his voice. "And the whole time we had our other relationship?"

Oh, god. I *did* trick him. I never thought of it like that, but we were supposed to be emotionally honest with each other as Dom and sub. "It was the whole time. But I didn't realize it until recently."

"You didn't realize you've been," he struggles with his words, "in love with me? Is that what you're saying here? That you're still in love with me?"

"Yes." Tears spring to my eyes, and my voice quivers, but I have to keep myself together. I have to. We're in public, and he's a celebrity. Even if the town is currently made up of something like eighty percent celebrity, I can't draw attention to him. Especially since if anything made it to the blogs or social media, Madison could see it.

Oh, god, Madison. Here's this young girl, and I'm telling her boyfriend that I'm in love with him. God, I'm a monster.

*He was your boyfriend first!* my ego rages, and I try to tamp it down.

"All of these years." He shakes his head. "And you were fine being with me, as long as it was on your terms."

"What? No. That is not what our arrangement was, at all."

"Then, what was it?" he demands, his voice raising enough that the couple at the next table sharply look our way. He lowers it again and leans in. "Because, right now, what I'm hearing is that you held me at arm's length for six years while I pined for you—"

"Pined for me?" The hope that flares in my stomach makes it go sour. How can I feel victorious about this confirmation of his feelings when they're coming from such a place of hurt?

"Oh, come on," he scoffs. "You knew that I was still in love with you—"

"I didn't!" God, this is going so wrong. If I'd written this scene, we would fall into each other's arms, right now, then cut away to us getting married or something.

Oh, yeah, this is the perfect time to start imagining *that*.

Especially, since he seems mad enough to never speak to me, again. "How could you not? For six years, I didn't seriously date anyone else, because I was craving this thing I had with you. Because I couldn't give you up. And, now, I just feel used. If you were in love with me, we could have had something."

"We did have something. And it didn't work out," I remind him. My chest is tight. I think of all those times I Googled female symptoms of heart attacks.

"It didn't work out because you dumped me. You wanted to build your career on your own," he snarls. "And then, you kept working with me, anyway. You didn't have a fucking clue what you wanted."

He stands so abruptly that I jump, and the people around us look uncomfortable. Jack stalks out of the restaurant, leaving me behind. I don't care if it's technically a dine-and-dash since they're already making our food. I storm after him.

We're barely past the hostess stand when I catch up.

"You're right!" Fuck the stares of the other patrons. If Jack wants to have this fight, we'll do it right here, right now. "I didn't know what I wanted *six years ago*! Six years! And let's not forget that, when we broke up, I'd worked on one film. One. That you bought from me when I was still working as a professional dominatrix. Let's not pretend that we were on equal footing when it came to Hollywood savvy. I was trying to do what was best for me!"

"Like I never did anything that was best for you?" He stuns me into silence with that one. "And, in those intervening six years, you were what? Just waiting for the right moment to spring this on me?"

"No. I never meant to spring it on you. I was enjoying six years with my best friend. I didn't even realize that was what love is." My throat dries up.

He takes a step toward me, his expression dark and serious. "If you didn't know that was love, then how will you know when we're together, again?"

When? Again?

I sway on my feet, my body pulling toward his; the air between us has a weight to it. "You didn't know I loved you. But I didn't know you loved me, either. Now, we both know."

We stand in place, not saying a word. It's out, now.

"So, we've been in love this whole time. And we both managed to miss it."

The words are barely out of his mouth before it's on mine, right there in the hotel lobby. His arms are around my waist, pulling me tight against him. There are six years of kisses we could have had rolled into a sweet, passionate, lingering one that's not appropriate for public consumption.

"Is that Jack Martin?" a woman says, nearby. "I thought he was dating that *Beautiful Darkness* girl."

I push back, my face hot, my head dizzy. "Oh, shit."

"Yeah, this isn't…" He glances away, his jaw working. "We can't do this here."

We can't do this *here*. Not we can't do this. As if in confirmation, he takes my hand and pulls me toward the exit.

March 24, 2012

We're on my couch, watching a screener of some train wreck of a movie that Jack thinks is brilliant. To him, every gritty crime drama is *Chinatown*. I'm only acquiescing to this one because it's his birthday.

In the kitchen, the microwave dings, and he reluctantly pushes himself up from the couch. "Pause it?"

"Yeah." I click the button on the remote and get up to follow him. "I need a refill, too."

"And a break from the tough guys?" he teases. "I know this isn't your thing. I appreciate you tolerating this for me."

"I'm just sorry your big plans got ruined." Who the hell breaks up with someone the weekend before their birthday? Apparently, Jack's ex. They'd planned to go away to Catalina, but she called it off the night before the trip. She didn't even leave him with enough time to cancel the reservation.

"They didn't get ruined. They got altered." He opens the microwave and pulls out the popcorn bag. "And this way more fun than three days of nonstop sex."

I roll my eyes. "Sure, it is."

"Hey, my back ain't what it used to be. Not after that stupid chair stunt." He shakes his head.

"You should have left that to the professionals. They get paid to jump off houseboats while tied to chairs." I go the cupboard and reach for a bowl.

"This is a perfectly good bag right here," he informs me around a mouthful of popcorn.

"This way you don't get your whole hand greasy." I snatch the bag from him and empty it into the bowl, while he leans against the counter and watches in judgement. "And don't try to pretend that watching a DVD with your ex is a suitable substitute for nonstop sex. You're not making me feel better."

"Oh, cry me a river over your one-month dry spell." He takes the bowl from me. "Call me when it's been six months."

"No offense, but if it's been six months, I'm going to call someone I can have sex with." That person is not Jack.

He doesn't respond, right away. "Don't you miss it, though?"

"Sex?"

"Our sex."

*Our*? That's a weird thing to bring up. We haven't even been broken up for a full year, and he wants to talk about past sexual exploits? "Don't take this the wrong way, but you were good. Just not relapse good."

"Yikes, you make me sound like cancer." He grabs us two more beers, and we head to the living room. As we drop onto the couch, he adds, "I'm not fishing for birthday sex. I'm just curious. Was Dan into what we were into?"

I suck in a breath through my teeth. What Jack and I were "into" wasn't exactly something that would click with every guy. "What? Bondage? Domination? No, he was more of a let-me-worship-your-body type."

"He never let you tie him up?" Jack asks, shoving more popcorn into his mouth.

I shook my head. "Not even anything like a blindfold. He legitimately was not into it. And that was fine. I can live without it."

"I can't," Jack says, almost sadly. "Sex with Vanessa was okay. I mean, I got off. But it never felt as connected."

"That's because Doms and subs have a different kind of intimacy. Like, when I was doing it professionally, I had some repeat customers that I was really fond of. I didn't fall in love with them, but I definitely felt a little sad when I left. It's not like you get to hang out with guys normally after you've rubbed sandpaper on their dicks."

"Jesus Christ!" Jack exclaims. "Sandpaper?"

"Some guys are into that. Really fine-grade sandpaper, right on the head." I love watching Jack squirm at the thought.

And I realize that, yeah, I actually do miss tying him down and making him beg, even though I don't miss dating him.

It's not that different from those regular clients back in the day. I would never have dated any of the guys I Dommed for money—though a few had made sugar daddy offers I had a hard time resisting—but I clicked with some of them to the point that I really enjoyed myself. Not with all of them, but definitely with some of them.

I already know that I click with Jack.

"So, do you miss it?" I ask, propping my elbow on the back of the couch.

He nods. "I do. I don't think I've ever been as intimate with anyone as I was with you. Don't take this the wrong way, but that's actually the thing I miss most about us."

"Oh, sex? Yeah, that can't possibly be misconstrued."

"No, not the sex. The having something special that I never had with anyone else." He makes a frustrated noise as he searches for a way to explain. "Look, if it had been with anyone else, I don't think I would have felt that way. It was about trust. I trusted you, and it felt good to let my guard down like that."

"I can see that," I concede.

"What did you like about it?"

That's a loaded question. What am I supposed to say? That I get off on controlling men, sexually humiliating them, torturing them, and there's no deeper meaning to it? Put that way, I sound like a serial killer, even to myself. I've spent plenty of time trying to figure out why I like something so "perverted". No one, not even me, ever seemed content to just accept that it was something I liked, without any dirty secrets or childhood trauma involved.

"It's the power, I guess." I shrug, too embarrassed to meet his eyes. "I like knowing that you're never going to feel as good as I make you feel."

"Wow," he says with a chuckle. "That's bleak. But you might be right."

The memory of his skin, covered in a sheen of glittering sweat, the feeling of his muscles flexing and straining beneath it overwhelms me. I flush from the point of my v-neck t-shirt, all the way up to my face. I really hope he doesn't look down, because he'll see how erect my nipples are.

I can't help myself. "You know, it doesn't have to be something we never, ever do again."

His pulse shows in his pupils as he stares silently at me.

I squirm. "If you ever wanted to. When you're over me."

"When I'm over you?" He grins and shakes his head. "My, my. You *are* full of yourself tonight."

Oh, god. He's mad. I think.

"I didn't think you were the kind of girl who sleeps with her exes."

"Well, I'm not," I say firmly. I loved having sex with Jack, but sex leads to emotional messiness when you start involving people you used to be in love with. It's too easy for your body to forget what you're supposed to be feeling, and then, it drags your heart over the cliff with it. "I wouldn't have sex with you."

He sits up a little straighter. "You're serious."

"Yeah, absolutely." I try to sound friendly. Like I'm offering to help him move in exchange for a case of beer. "We're friends. It's not like we can't still have that intimacy as Dom and sub. It just won't be with a side of romance."

Now, he looks a lot more serious. He chews his thumbnail, his brow furrowed, expression inscrutable. When he takes a deep breath, I'm afraid he's been considering how to let me down. I never expect him to say, "I hired someone."

"Like, a professional?" My eyebrows have vanished into my hairline, I'm sure. I hope he realizes that I'm not being judgmental. And I'm not shocked that a guy in Hollywood hired a sex worker. But I *am* shocked that it's Jack. He's so private and distant until he gets to know someone. "How did that go?"

"Not well. I couldn't quite…get there." He quickly adds, "Not orgasm. I mean, she got me off. But I didn't get to that subspace. Something was just hanging on."

"So, it *is* the trust, then." I nod thoughtfully, like I'm BDSM Oprah or something.

"It is. And that's not something you can just spring on someone the first time you have sex. 'By the way, would you mind strapping me down and rubbing sandpaper on my dick?'"

We both fall apart laughing, and it breaks the tension, at least for long enough that the air comes back to the room.

"I wasn't kidding," I tell him. "If you ever want to, we can. It would be up to you."

He reaches for the remote to start up the movie, but pauses before he hits the button. With a sly grin, he looks over at me and asks, "Do Tuesdays work for you?"

Jenny Trout

## Chapter Twelve

We crash through the door of Jack's suite and don't wait for the door to click shut before we're tearing at each other's clothes. We didn't talk in his hired car on the way over; there wasn't a partition, and I think we just didn't want to break the spell. If we did, we would have to think about the real world. Like we would talk ourselves out of it, or find out that our loose ends just can't be tied up.

If I have to learn more knots than a sailor, I'm going to make sure they *are* tied up.

Our coats fall on the floor. I push my hands under his sweater and force it up. He takes it off the rest of the way, and the t-shirt underneath it, too. My shirt comes off, and he fumbles with the clasp of my bra, not because he doesn't know what he's doing, but because his hands are shaking. I feel them tremble as he skates his palms down my sides.

We manage all of this between kisses, our lips meeting desperately and automatically as breathing. His mouth slides up my jaw to my ear, and I stumble backward. The wall catches me, and Jack does, too, pressing me hard against it with his body. His skin is hot and soft against mine, and I want to touch it all.

But he wants to touch me more. It's been longer for him. I've been over every inch of him, more than once. I've made him experience unbelievable pleasure almost every Tuesday night for the past five years, but he's never been able to return that. The whole time, it was a part of the torment, and we both knew that.

He pushes his hand into the front of my jeans, and the button pops to let him in. He can't reach too far, but his fingertips brush my pubic hair, and that's enough to make him groan. "Do you know how long it's been since I've been inside you?"

*Six years.* I didn't realize I was keeping track.

With a growl of frustration, he jerks my pants down far enough to touch the wet, hot flesh between my thighs. He slips one finger into my cunt, and I gasp, clutching on him. He leans his forehead against mine, slowly drawing his finger out and spreading the wetness over my clit. "Let me have you tonight," he pleads. "Let have all of you."

I swallow, and nod, because my voice isn't working. Not with his finger swirling around and around, touching me where no one has touched me in a really, *really* long time. He keeps stroking me as he lowers his head to kiss down the side of my neck, over my collarbones. I rock my hips, riding his hand as his mouth finds one of my nipples, and I come, shuddering and moaning.

"It's been too long since I've heard that." He laughs, withdrawing his hand. He steadies me as I toe off my shoes and kick my jeans aside. I move to take a step, but he stops me, pinning me to the wall, again, as he works his belt buckle. We're both buck naked, and we haven't even made it to the bedroom, yet.

He kisses me, leaning against me so we're skin-to-skin from hip to chest, and raises my leg to fit around his waist. His cock is hard between us, and he grinds it against me, rocking the length along my slit. I rub shamelessly on him, hoping he'll give in and just slip inside. But, when he breaks the kiss, he releases me and takes my hands to pull me to the bedroom.

The massive California king dominates the spacious room. Jack must have paid a fortune for a suite this big. "Come on, get up," he says, almost pushing me onto the bed, and I fall, laughing breathlessly. He kneels between my legs and holds my thighs open with a hand on each, spreading me wide. I want to watch as he lowers his mouth to my sex, but the anticipation is too much, and my eyelids flutter closed. The first wet, delicious touch drags a long breath from me, and I lick my lips. His tongue is so warm and soft as it teases up and down my labia. My pussy clenches and floods, and I arch my back, trying to force harder contact. But he takes his time with teasing glides of his flattened tongue that sweep upward from my cunt, almost to where I want to feel him. It's a fitting and beautiful revenge for the past five years of teasing that I put him through. If only I were more patient, so I could appreciate the divine justice.

I'm anything but patient, and he has to hold me still as I whimper and writhe until, finally, he burrows his tongue between my labia and circles my clit. He releases one of my thighs to slide his hand down and penetrate me with one finger. He remembers exactly where to go. My knees hug his head, and my heels drum the small of his back. Jack understands how to eat a woman out; he finds the right pattern, and he sticks with it until I'm shrieking and shaking and clawing the duvet.

He lifts his head and says, dismayed, "I don't have any condoms. Please tell me you've still got that IUD thing."

I laugh breathlessly. "Yes, I still have that IUD thing."

"Oh, thank god." He lunges up my body, settling between my legs and grasping my wrists to bring them above my head, where he holds them with one hand. My body is stretched and vulnerable beneath him. With another person, that would make me uncomfortable. But this is Jack. I can't think of anyone else in the world who I trust more.

There's no moment of awkwardness or difficulty when he slides himself inside of me. Our bodies recognize each other. They've memorized each other. And, when he's in me, filling me, he stays there, holding me down, searching my eyes, his need apparent.

"I love you," he says, never breaking my gaze as he grows restless inside me.

Overwhelmed by sensation, I tip my head back and moan, "I love you, too."

He strokes slowly in and out, and we savor every ripple, every throb. My knees come up to bracket his waist, to draw him in deeper. He releases my arms, and they find their way around him, too, my hands roaming over his shoulders, his back, the muscles flexing beneath my palms. I've been with guys who were in great shape and thought that was the only thing they had to bring to the table, sexually. But Jack uses his body like a sexual athlete, every movement fluid and purposeful. He's not just strong. He's *skilled*.

I move right along with him, in a rhythm that rises and falls, driven by an intimate communication neither of us has to speak aloud. Our breaths and moans keep the tempo, guiding us from slow and measured to frantic and pounding, both of us straining together to go deeper, faster, to exert ourselves until we're absolutely depleted.

This was why we couldn't have made our "just friends" arrangement work if we kept having sex. It was never just sex with us. It's always a sweet trial, a passionate ordeal. Tonight, we fuck like it's the last time and the first time. We make it count.

"I'm almost there," he warns me, taking one of my hands to guide it between us. I reach between us and swirl my fingertips over my clit, but the position makes it awkward.

"Wait." I wriggle back, and he moans as he slips from my body. Whatever, he's used to getting close and being denied. He'll live. I roll over and get on my hands and knees, and he doesn't miss the invitation. He fills me while I touch myself, and I can tell he won't be long. "Don't stop," I urge.

"I can't..." His sweat drips onto my back as he drives deep, pulsing inside me with a tortured groan. The twitch of his cock as he comes is unmistakable.

"I said don't stop," I order, knowing that the tone of my voice alone will make him go on. Conditioned by half a decade of sexual subservience, he keeps fucking me. He begs and whines and curses at me, and those pathetic whimpers drive me higher and higher. Knowing how sensitive he is, how excruciating this must be, how much willpower he exerts over his body to force himself to obey spins me out of control, and I pump my hips faster, dragging out the torment as I come with a long wail of satisfaction.

He doesn't stop until I tell him to.

We roll apart, wilting into the mattress beside each other. I lift my hand to run it through my sweat-damp hair, but he catches it and brings my fingertips to his lips. "I love you."

"Yeah, you mentioned that," I tease, a tired smile stretching my face. We don't speak for long time, our heavy breathing the only sound.

Finally, he says, in a voice that sounds as if he desperately needs water, "You're still a sick bitch in bed, you know that?"

We both laugh, and I reach out as though I'll grab his cock. His body jerks to defend itself, and I lay back, throwing an arm over my head on the pillow.

"Yeah, I know," I admit, stretching everything, right down to my toes. "And I know you like it."

"I do." He rolls to his side and gazes down at me for a long moment, his eyes drifting to the scar on my forehead. All the humor drains from his expression, and he grows serious. "I quit the sequel."

"What?" I force myself up on my elbows. "You can't quit, can you? You're the producer."

"Not of *Beautiful Lightness*. We were supposed to go into negotiations for the next one, but all that plagiarism stuff came up. Plus, I was told in no uncertain terms that Lynn would have the final word in every decision. I said I couldn't work like that."

"Nobody can." I pity whoever takes over. "Is she writing the screenplay?"

"Probably. Some of the cast is threatening to walk, too. They didn't sign on for sequels, and the experience shooting the movie was… I mean, Madison has already said she won't do another." His eyes go wide with horror. He flops back on the pillows and covers his face. "Oh, my god. Madison."

My heart lurches. If he changes his mind, now, if he dashes the hopes he just raised…

There's no way I won't cause some sort of epic sobbing scene. I bite the inside of my cheek to keep premature tears at bay.

"I should have probably broken up with her before." He scrubs his hands down, and the expression revealed is grim and resolved. "I'll talk to her when I get back. I'm not going to mention this." He waves in the space between us.

"No, there's no reason to." It would be needlessly cruel. If Jack feels guilty about it, that's something he's just going to have to live with. And I'm callous and selfish enough that I don't really care about the ethics of him fucking me while still dating another woman, as long as he's choosing me in the end.

"I still feel like an asshole." He reaches out to touch my lower lip with his thumb. "But I'm not sorry."

I wriggle closer to him and lay my head in the crook of his shoulder and chest. "When do you go back to L.A.?"

"Tomorrow afternoon. What about you?"

"Day after tomorrow." I feel so warm and relaxed that the thought of ever standing up again is unbearable.

He makes a disappointed noise. "Do you want to fly home with me? I've got a charter. I won't even make you split the fare."

"No way." I pick his hand up and weave our fingers together over his chest. "Sherri and I are going to a party. I heard that Sting might be there."

"I guess that's a good enough reason to stay," he says, adding, "It'll give me a chance to break up with Madison."

I don't really want to know the answer, but I ask, anyway. "Do you love her?"

He tilts his head and frowns at the ceiling. "Yeah. I do. And it sucks that I let her down. But I love you a hell of a lot more."

A fleeting stab of panic pierces me. What if he goes back to California, sees Madison, and realizes this is all a mistake? But that seems too ridiculous to bother worrying about. Jack isn't going to go back to Madison. Whatever's happened between us tonight feels permanent.

Still, I roll onto my side and lean up on my elbow to look down at him. "You know that I belong to you, right?"

"No." He reaches up to sink a hand in my hair and drags me down. In the moment before his lips meet mine, he whispers, "If anyone belongs to anyone here, I belong to you."

Jenny Trout

January 25, 2017

**IT'S OVER!**

Things might have gotten too dark on the troubled set of *Beautiful Darkness*. Amid the delays in production and behind-the-scenes strife, actress Madison Avery has announced the end of her whirlwind romance with actor and producer Jack Martin. In a statement released through her publicist, Avery praises Martin for "teaching me the value of honesty and always treating me with respect".

The pair only dated for four months, but according to a source close to the actress, Avery is "devastated" by the breakup. "He was her first love," the source tells *TSW*. "She's not going to get over him that easily."

Rumors are still flying about an alleged on-set romance between Avery and her hunky costar, Wren Taylor, but there's no word on whether or not their alleged relationship was a cause of her breakup with Martin. What we do know is that this could make for an interesting red carpet premiere, and you can count on *TSW* to bring you all the details.

## Epilogue

It's so childish of me to scour social media for details about the premiere, but here I am, sitting on the couch, laptop across my thighs, every hashtag possible open in different browser tabs.

I was not invited. In fact, the studio asked me specifically not to come, and not to comment on the premiere. I wouldn't have wanted to go, anyway. Staying as far away from Lynn Baldwin as possible is my new life goal. But I still want the dirt.

Red carpet photos are starting to pop up on Twitter. The Mistress of Darkness herself has shown up sans date; I read somewhere that her husband really did run off with Kathy Muller, after all. Someone designed a dress for Lynn that's fitting of a Disney villainess, a slinky dark-red number with an overlay of sheer black material speckled with sequins. I wonder how many enormous tantrums she threw at the designer.

There's one of Madison Avery posing beside Wren. She's wearing a pale peach halter-neck dress that practically matches her skin tone, and bright red lipstick that's more trendy than suits her. Wren is back to his usual too-cool style, rocking ripped jeans and a purple paisley blazer over his white shirt and bow tie. For some reason, he's grown a wild bushy beard that obscures most of his face.

I head over to *They Said What?* and click on their live feed. There's Madison, again, and Wren, with Lynn and Marion and Jack. All of them stand at awkward intervals. They're supposed to look like friends and coworkers, but the flashes of the cameras might as well be bullets from a firing squad from the looks on their faces.

"Oh," I say, drawing the word out with affectionate dismay as I watch Jack try hard to keep his smile as he and

Marion flank Lynn. He's been dreading this premiere all day, pacing the house in a big ball of tension.

I check the time in the corner of the screen and force myself to close my browser. If I'm going to hit my word count goal for the day, I need to take advantage of the time I have. Writing a novel is completely different from writing a screenplay. I can't just rely on the director and producer to figure out which way to shoot the scene, which way the characters should deliver lines. I'm making an entire movie myself, to be projected into a totally unique, isolated audience's head.

But I love it. I love knowing that I'm not going to have to brace myself to hear my words read aloud in a room full of people who are there to be critical. I love knowing that no absolutely evil person with a gargantuan ego is going to hurl objects at me if she deems my work subpar.

And I never, ever have to go back to that life if I don't want to.

I write until the alarm on my phone goes off. I saved myself an hour to get ready.

I go to the closet and pull out my new favorite outfit. It's sheer gold-tinted latex with strategic slashes of wide black asymmetrical stripes and a big bow on the single shoulder strap. Dramatic dresses go well with dramatic makeup, so I smoke up my eyes and slick on a dark lip gloss.

I'm waiting in the entryway when Jack rings the doorbell. He has a key; it's his house. Or, our house, now, even though I'm still getting used to saying that. But we have plans tonight.

He steps inside and shuts the door. The latch clicks in the silence.

I look to the clock on the wall. "You're late."

"I'm sorry, Mistress." He pulls his untied bowtie from his collar and drops it and his jacket on the floor.

"Three minutes." I tsk and turn away, heading for our kink room. "You know what that means."

"Yes, Mistress," he says.

Though I don't look over my shoulder, I know he's following me.

FADE OUT

## Also by Jenny Trout

### Writing as Abigail Barnette:

Bad Boy, Good Man
Surrender

## THE SOPHIE SCAIFE SERIES

The Stranger
The Boss
The Girlfriend
The Bride
The Ex
The Baby

## THE BY-THE-NUMBERS SERIES

First Time (Penny's Story)
First Time (Ian's Story)
Second Chance (Penny's Story)
Second Chance (Ian's Story)

## THE CANIS CLAN SERIES:

Bride Of The Wolf
Wolf's Honor

### Writing as Jenny Trout

Choosing You

**Jenny Trout** is an author, blogger, and funny person. Jenny made the *USA Today* bestseller list with her debut novel, *Blood Ties Book One: The Turning.* Her *American Vampire* was named one of the top ten horror novels of 2011 by *Booklist* Magazine Online. As Abigail Barnette, Jenny writes award-winning erotic romance, including the internationally bestselling *The Boss* series.

As a blogger, Jenny's work has appeared on *The Huffington Post*, and has been featured on television and radio, including *HuffPost Live*, *Good Morning America*, *The Steve Harvey Show*, and National Public Radio's *Here & Now*. Her work has earned mentions in *The New York Times* and *Entertainment Weekly*.

She is a proud Michigander, mother of two, and wife to the only person alive capable of spending extended periods of time with her without wanting to kill her.

22469636R00126

Printed in Great Britain
by Amazon